KATHY

5
things

LESSONS FROM BOAZ
ON HOW TO LOVE WELL

REVISED EDITION
WITH DISCUSSION QUESTIONS

EQ STUDIO PUBLISHING

5 Things
Copyright ©2014 by Kathy B. Nelson. All rights reserved.

ISBN: 978-1-63306-024-1
Published by EQ Studio Publishing
104 School Street Youngsville LA 70592 337.573.9100
www.eqstudio.net
Book design copyright ©2019 by Miriam Douglas.

DEDICATION

To my *Daughters* Katie Garcia and Lisa Ellon Stapp, for being personal cheerleaders on this journey with me. Always encouraging. Thank you for loving Jesus. Thank you for giving us amazing, fun grandchildren.

To my *Mother*, June Brabham, for being a faithful example of how teaching God's word never gets old or boring no matter what age you are teaching. Thank you for your tireless and devoted life and love for missions. You are an example of being 'all in' for the most important things.

To *Daddy*, who is in his heavenly home now. Thank you for leaving a legacy of humor, a contagious love for all people, a faithfulness to God, and the local church. Those gifts have made my life so much richer and so much more fun.

To my *Husband* Rick for his help in getting this project done. Thank you for supporting me, both times.

To all of my *Friends* for helping me believe I could actually do this and encouraging me to not be afraid.

To all of the *college students, youth, single adults, married couples*, and *parents*. You inspired the first edition and now you have inspired this second edition of 5 Things. I will forever be grateful for the mark you have left in my life.

Acknowledgements

To my Redeemer, Jesus Christ, for being the ultimate and ever-present subject in this book. Your redemption has been the sustaining act in all of my life. Thank you for loving me, so I can love you back.

For the precious, powerful, life giving word of God

"For the word of God is quick, and powerful, and sharper than any two-edged sword, piercing even to the dividing asunder of soul and spirit, and of the joints and marrow, and is a discerner of the thoughts and intents of the heart."
Hebrews 4:12 (KJV)

Katie Garcia, Lisa Stapp, Melissa Sullivan, Sandy Allen and Helene Shaw, for the time spent helping me put the words I have spoken to words on a page. Your insights and academic excellence have been priceless.

Sarah Doss – for editing a book that needed much work and making me feel confident in releasing this new edition. What a gifted editor you are!

CONTENTS

CHAPTER ONE:
Count the Cost

"If you do not carry your own cross and follow me, you cannot be my disciple. But don't begin until you count the cost. For who would begin construction of a building without first calculating the cost to see if there is enough money to finish it? Otherwise, you might complete only the foundation before running out of money, and then everyone would laugh at you. They would say, 'There's the person who started that building and couldn't afford to finish it!' Or what king would go to war against another king without first sitting down with his counselors to discuss whether his army of 10,000 could defeat the 20,000 soldiers marching against him? And if he can't he will send a delegation to discuss terms of peace while the enemy is still far away. So you cannot become my disciple without giving up everything you own."

Luke 14: 27-33

The best marriage relationship are made up of faithful disciples of Christ. Those who have counted the cost and chosen to start building under the direction of the Master Builder himself. Those who are ready and equipped to finish the tower. Free to choose whether to begin a committed relationship, but not free from cost. Have you counted the cost of investing in the life of someone else?

Marriage is like a tower. Building this marriage tower will involve patience in dating and find its completion in a marriage that lasts a lifetime. My hope in this book is to give guys and girls some absolutely critical tools for the construction and completion of the marriage tower.

But first, maybe it is time for everyone to sit down and see if you have what it takes to finish this tower. Do you want to start building this tower beginning with dating and ending with a life-long marriage? Have you considered what the cost is to finish this ultimate tower, the marriage tower? Are you committed to following the blueprints that God has established regarding these relationship and how God command you to love and conduct yourself in them? King David begged the Lord to show him what he needed to change in his life;

"O Lord, you have examined my heart and know everything about me. You know when I sit down or stand up. You know my thoughts even when I'm far away. You see me when I travel and when I rest at home. You know everything I do. Search me, O God, and know my heart; test me and know my anxious thought. Point out anything in me that offends you and lead me along the path of everlasting life." Psalm 139:1-3, 23-24

Do you need to do the same? Consider taking some time this week in prayer, asking God to show you the things in your life that you might need to change.

After 30 years of working with young adults in ministry, I know there are still guys and girls who want to grow to spiritual maturity. God places within everyone, at creation, the need to be like him because everyone was created his image. And because you were created in his image, you will need to go the source of instruction for how to live this life from your Creator. The bible reveals how God has de-

signed you and what he require of
you. We see very quickly that be-
cause of sin, we cannot do anything
good on our own.

God's word also provides the
fundamental blueprint for how to
build relationships, grow in love
and marry wisely. Being grounded
and equipped in the word of God by
memorizing and applying it do our
lives – which mean obeying – not only helps us make wise choice in
dating and marriage, but God's word serves as a lamp to our feet and
a light to our path for the future. Hiding God's word in our hearts
enables us to live in the fullness of life that God so wants to give us
whether we marry or not. Let us acknowledge that becoming like
Jesus is always the end goal, not getting married.

Inevitably, in the future, you will encounter instruction about
marriage and relationships from a conference speaker, a book or a
magazine article. As you are working through these resources, ask
yourself if what you are reading or being taught is in God's word.
Any expectation that is set for you that is less than, or in addition to,
God's standard is temporary and may even be counter to a lifetime
commitment of marriage. Weigh each suggestion and determine if it
is a principle or precept from God's word. If it is lacking in biblical
credibility, then consider it someone's opinion and therefore, not a
mandate from God. Don't waste your time trying to shore up your
heart on things that are not eternal.

Effective, fulfilling and enduring relationships will come when people first live out their faith in Christ, being obedient to his commands on their life. Great relationships and great marriages cannot depend on the changing preferences of surveys, trendy relationship experts or popular opinions. These preferences teach us about the culture we live in, but they cannot teach us truths of eternal value. Not only that, I believe the culture's influence has in some ways crippled us with shallow rules, minimal expectations and flesh-driven requirements.

Brothers and Sisters I Christ, you have access to all of God's power as a resource for all matters of your life. Because God is love, you can love. If you have trusted Jesus and committed your life to follow him, you have the Holy Spirit living within you. His Spirit enables you to love like God does, just like Jesus did when he was here on earth. When you have counted the cost of trusting Christ and obeying his instructions in all matters of life, he will guide you to all truth.

Tremendous peace and security is present when a girl is willing to wait to date a guy that is trusting God and obeying His commands. Even if such a dating relationship doesn't evolve into marriage, hopefully she has developed a wonderful friendship, and those are truly rare. Be ever so thankful for a Godly friend. If a husband is willing to die for his wife, to sacrifice his life for her like Jesus did for his Bride, which is the Church, maybe a guy needs to first

4

count the cost for building this tower.

Scripture teaches that your days are numbered and only God knows the length of them, so it is urgent that you redeem the time you have on this earth and make it count for eternity. Give God's relationship plan a chance. Marriage will always involve a measure of faith. No potential mate will ever be perfect. Marriage is a commitment to someone for the rest of your life, so make wise decisions before you ever date someone. Surely it can't hurt to give God's plan a try. Find some people around you that love Jesus and are devoted to becoming like him and let them help you build this tower. You need them and they can help you.

LET'S PRAISE GOD FOR ESTABLISHING A COVENANT RELATIONSHIP WITH US THAT MAKES GODLY RELATIONSHIPS POSSIBLE. AND, LET'S OPEN UP THE BLUEPRINTS FOR THIS MARRIAGE TOWER AND LEARN MORE OF GOD'S PLAN FOR RELATIONSHIPS.

CHAPTER ONE:
DISCUSSION QUESTIONS

1. *What is some relationship advice you typically read in magazines, see on TV or read on social media?*

2. *List 4 truths regarding God's commands for a marriage, and the scripture reference that teaches that truth.*

       1.

       2.

       3.

       4.

3. *What are some ways you see your behavior or relationship goals reflecting Jesus?*

What are some areas of your behavior in relationships that need to be transformed or matured to be more like Christ?

4. *In the space below, sketch out a tower with the foundation and each layer of support named a virtue that you think is critical for a relationship tower to stand.*

Why did you choose the virtues for the foundation?

Was there a reason for the order that you put them?

CHAPTER TWO:
To the Men of God

Men of God, I am a fan. God created men to be the head of our households and I am so thankful for that plan. God has designed men in His image and can equip each man with all that he needs to fulfill this role.

This book is designed to help you learn 5 things – basically five primary disciplines that guys should develop in their lives. Don't settle for the character traits that the world suggests. These worldly traits are designed to fulfill temporary wants and appeal to the selfish desire of your mind and bodies. They seem fulfilling for a season, but ultimately leave you empty and disillusioned.

Brothers in Christ, choosing to have a standard of Godliness in your dating relationships is going to require a lot from you in discipline, patience and service. Ephesians 5:25 tells husbands to love their wives just like Christ also loved the church and gave himself up for her. Jesus' plan is not an easy path. When he calls a man to lead his home by loving his wife, serving her, and being willing to die for her, he has set the cost of that tower pretty high.

I fear that we have done men a disservice in our culture today. Guys are designed to be more than the sum of a survey. However, the "ideal" for a man has been so dumbed down and stereotyped through media, music, and even some faith-based relationship ex-

9

perts, it's no wonder we have men tripping over the proverbial bar that has been set at about his knees.

If one more person says that inappropriate, unethical, lustful, rude, thoughtless, ungodly behavior in men should be understood, I am going to scream. Furthermore, if the suggested response to these bad behaviors is that the girlfriend or wife should change something to accommodate the man's behavior because he is "hard-wired" in a certain way, then we need to flip on the switch of the Light of the World to expose the ridiculousness and foolishness of this claim.

The truth is everyone is "hard-wired" for bad behavior. It's called sin. Romans 3:23 says everyone has missed the mark that God intended for people. He also teaches that the way people used to think and be motivated must be offered as a sacrifice to God, so that your desires and motivations may be controlled by the Spirit of God. You need to surrender to this plan of God in every area of your life.

This "hard-wired" excuse runs pretty shallow. If guys are lusting after girls, it does not mean their girlfriend, or wife, should start dressing cuter, lose some weight, or workout more so they won't be tempted to lust. A guy is solely responsible for his choices. Every individual is responsible for their choices. If lust has taken him captive, then he must repent and stop lusting.

God says, "But I say, anyone who even looks at a woman with lust has already committed adultery with her in his heart." Matthew 5:28. So, by the mercies of God, don't buy into this spineless philosophy that a guy's girlfriend, or wife, must adjust when he has been caught in sin. Reject the lies expectations are too high when others expect faithfulness and integrity in a man's life. Rebuke the lies that a guy's bad-boy, "hard-wired" behavior should be tolerated and understood, when the mercy and grace of our Redeemer implores you to repent.

notes:

If a guy is a born-again Christian, his behavior is weighed and measured by the plumb line of God's word alone, not a result of anyone else's survey, opinions, or cultural norms. There are guys who don't want God to find them lacking in the spiritual maturity it takes to build a healthy relationship into a lifetime marriage. It's time to grow up. It's time to live out God's commands on your life.

A guy must determine in his heart today to fulfill what God has planned for him. A girl needs him to do that. The whole world needs you to fulfill that plan, not due to popular vote, but because it is God's divine order.

A guy's transformation from what he used to be and how he used to think can only take place by the power of Almighty God. It's like when babies know only the inside of a warm and safe womb and them bam! lights, coldness and a slap on the behind welcome them to this new life in the world! They will see, hear, and feel things they never have before. That's what happens when the scales of your spiritually blinded eyes are removed. What seemed safe, logical, and predictable changes. These new, unveiled eyes reveal that he has this heart that can be hurt and wounded. But, men's hearts also have this enormous capacity for love, favor, commitment, grace, forgiveness, joy and so much more. These attributes are not possible because he has it within his own power to demonstrate them, but because God gives them to him and empowers him, through his Holy Spirit, to sustain them.

There are legions of God's people who want to fight for every guy to be strong and faithful. Girls need to see guys stand firm and be strong in spirit and character so that she can be confident that one day he will take his place as the head of the household and be victorious as he positions himself on the front lines of protecting his family.

Guys who can, and will, count the cost for building the tower and find that he does indeed have what it takes to finish the construction of it should be cheered on and applauded by the family of God.

When you give away everything in order to be a disciple of Christ, then you begin to take on the characteristics of the only living, one-true God. I mean surrendering to God's plan and leading for your life. When you trust God's leading, you have this awareness within you that someone is bigger than you; someone is in control and making provision for you somehow. And that someone is Almighty God. Maybe that is why the most remote village where no civilized influence has been seen or felt will have a totem pole at the center of their village where people go to worship or a rock carved in the shape of some idol. They seem to have an awareness that there is someone they need to thank and therefore worth worshipping. In Acts 17, the Apostle Paul saw an altar to one of these "unknown gods" when he was traveling through Athens.

"So Paul, standing before the council, addressed them as follows: 'Men of Athens, I notice that you are very religious in every way, for as I was walking along I saw your many shrines. And one of your altars had this inscription on it: 'To an Unknown God.' This God, whom you worship without knowing, is the one I'm telling you about. He is the God who made the world and everything in it. Since he is Lord of heaven and earth, he doesn't live in man-made temples, and human hands can't serve his needs – for he has no needs. He himself gives life and breath to everything, and he satisfies every need."

Acts 17: 22-25

MEN OF GOD, ARE YOU WILLING TO COUNT THE COST TO
BUILD THE TOWER?
DO YOU DESIRE TO GROW INTO SPIRITUAL MATURITY SO
YOU CAN LEAD THOSE AROUND YOU WELL?

DISCUSSION QUESTIONS

1.   *What have you been told throughout your life that "real men" do?*

2.   *Why does God have an order in a marriage? How do you see your role?*

3.   *Where do you feel most challenged in the role God has placed you in the family?*

4.   *Think about your growing up years, and who raised you. What did you learn about being a husband or wife by watching them?*

What examples would you want to carry into your own relationships and marriage?

And which ones do you want to leave behind?

5. *Excuses can cripple us in our growth. What excuses have you given for your behavior that is not pleasing to the Lord?*

   How do you surrender those excuses to God so that he can transform your heart and thus transform your behavior?

6. *Have you been born-again? See Page 138 for help in knowing how you can be born again.*

   How has your life changed since you started following Jesus?

7. *Who, in your life, has been an encourager – someone who cheered you on – in your spiritual growth?*

16

CHAPTER THREE:
To the Women of God

Women of God, this book is designed to help you learn the 5 things as well. You need to know these 5 things that guys need to develop, and be demonstrating, in their lives so that you will know them when you see them demonstrated, but discipline yourself to wait for them. Don't let the world tell you what a godly man, or even just a good man, should look like.

When a girl desires to follow Christ, she should wait for a guy who is pursuing God's plan. She needs to wait for the guy who listens to and learns from those who would point him to Christ as the model for all of his behavior. Her self-imposed timelines of marriage need to be surrendered on the altar of God's perfect timing. You are so worth waiting for a man who will love you like Jesus does.

"You saw me before I was born. Every day of my life was recorded in your book. Every moment was laid out before a single day had passed."

Psalm 139:16

Girls should make decisions about who they will date based on the guy's character. The character you see right now lived out before you. Don't date someone hoping he will develop these disciplines later. When a girl waits for a guy that is displaying these attributes

17

she can have a greater confidence through faith that God will honor their relationship and, should it lead to marriage, God will sustain their marriage for a lifetime. It's not just a fairytale, lifetime marriages really can happen. Scripture command it, so God can enable it. Wait for God to do the work. Wait for a man in whom you can identify the development of the enduring character of God.

When a girl is willing to wait to date a guy that trusts God and obeys His commands, she'll experience tremendous peace and security in the relationship. Even if such a dating relationship doesn't evolve into marriage, hopefully, the two have developed a wonderful, healthy friendship. Be thankful for a good friend, they are so rare after a breakup.

Sisters in Christ, Ephesians 5:22 teaches wives to be submissive to their husbands, as you would be to the Lord. Here are a few questions you should ask yourself before committing to anyone in a dating relationship:

IS TRUSTING THIS MAN TO LEAD YOUR FAMILY ONE DAY
AN EASY THOUGHT?

DO YOU RESPECT THIS MAN ENOUGH TO
FOLLOW HIS LEAD IF YOU BECOME HIS WIFE?

IS HE A MAN THAT YOU WILL TRUST TO INFLUENCE
AND MOLD THE LIVES AND SPIRITS OF YOUR CHILDREN?

Your personal accountability before God will not be about what kind of husband he was, but about your obedience to the plan God has for you as his wife. You must surrender your own needs to the Lord and let God's plans become your plans.

notes:

Keep in mind, if the man that you love and think you want to marry, does not demonstrate these five disciplines are going to learn about, it doesn't mean he never will. What it does mean is that you need to wit. Girls, pray for the guy you love – or even better, pray for Christian guys to desire these disciplines and that God will work in their lives to develop them. If they don't have a relationship with Jesus Christ, pray for him to see his need for a Savior and give his life to Christ. Encouragement and respect can urge these great guys to want to grow in godliness. The same is true with a girl's disciplines as well.

In this time of life when she is not married, a girl should be focusing on her obedience to the mission that God has given her. She should grow and flourish in a life of surrender to the Lord. Every one of us was created with precision and care. God knew what each of us would look like and how many hairs would be on our head before we were ever born. We can trust God to guide our life and that includes our relationships.

Both women and men are created in the image of God and each have specific needs. How gracious and perfect of God to also create within men and women the ability to meet those needs for each other. How generous of God, our Creator, to make us all different in personality and gifting so that we can serve one another and love each other like he does.

WOMEN OF GOD, ARE YOU WILLING TO SURRENDER TO GOD IN YOUR RELATIONSHIP AND IN YOUR SPIRITUAL GROWTH? ARE YOU WILLING TO TRUST GOD FOR HIS BEST IN YOUR LIFE?

CHAPTER THREE:
DISCUSSION QUESTIONS

1. *What influences have you had that helped shape who you are and what you believe about women?*

2. *Why do you think bad behavior does not deter a dating relationship from forming?*

What light does the Bible shed on this tendency?

3. *Look up "submission" in the dictionary. What does it mean in this context?*

What does it NOT mean?

4. *What does the Bible teach us about personal responsibility?*

5. *List at least 5 ways Godly character can strengthen your relationships*

      1.

      2.

      3.

      4.

      5.

6. *List 5 ways the lack of Godly character can destroy or undermine a relationship*

      1.

      2.

      3.

      4.

      5.

7. *Why do you think it is hard to wait for someone to date that is Godly?*

What would it take to change that?

24

CHAPTER FOUR:
What is it About Boaz?

In my request to God for instruction and insight in how to equip the guys in our collegiate ministry to be Godly boyfriends and eventually great husbands, God sent me to the book of Ruth.

God spoke truth into my heart as I was reacquainted with the amazing relationship between Boaz and Ruth. I know these disciplines God pointed out to me are good because God wrote the book. And I know the disciplines demonstrated in the book of Ruth work, because God's ways work.

Ruth grew up in Moab. The family of Elimelech and Naomi moved to Moab from Bethlehem with their sons Mahlon and Chilion because there was a famine in Bethlehem. Ruth met and married Mahlon. His brother Chilion married a woman named Orpah. Tragically, all three of these men, Elimelech, the father, Mahlon and Chilion, all died while in Moab, leaving Naomi, Ruth and Orpah all widows. After living in Moab for about ten years, Naomi's deep grief and bitterness of heart after losing all the men in her family caused her to move back to Bethlehem in order to be closer to her family whom she loved. Naomi begged her daughter-in-law's to stay in Moab and find another husband among their people, but Ruth insisted on moving to Bethlehem with her. Ruth felt very committed to Naomi and wanted to help her any way she could. She had also developed a loyalty to the God that Naomi worshipped and served. Jehovah God became her Lord. Her statement of commitment to Naomi has been used in many wedding ceremonies as part of the vows that are made: "But Ruth replied, 'Don't ask me to leave you and turn back. Wherever you go, I will go; wherever you live, I will live. Your people will be my people, and your God will be my God.'" Ruth 1:16

Ruth, herself, is worthy to be studied and learned from; however, it is from the example of Boaz that these five disciplines for guys to incorporate in their life were developed.

Ram was the father of Amminadab, Amminadab was the father of Nahshon. Nahshon was the father of Salmon. Salmon was the father of Boaz (whose mother was Rahab). Boaz was the father of Obed (whose mother was Ruth). Obed was the father of Jesse. Jesse was the father of King David. David was the father of Solomon (whose mother was Bathsheba, the widow of Uriah).

Matthew 1:4-6

Boaz's mother, Rahab, was a prostitute. Imagine that. Right there in the lineage of Christ is a woman that no one would expect to be there. Would anyone believe that a man like Boaz, who the bible teaches in the book of Ruth, loved so purely and was such a respected man in the community- and yes, a man who loved the Lord God so faithfully- would be the son of a prostitute?

The fact that Boaz's mother, Rahab was a prostitute points us to God's grace, mercy, and unconditional love already. What a glorious message of hope for guys and girls everywhere. No matter the upbringing or lack of instruction in spiritual things, even to the point

notes:

of your home life being the exact opposite of what God desires it to be, God can and will redeem it when you put your faith in Him. When Rahab trusted the God of Israel in the book of Joshua, Chapter 2, God turned her whole life around. From a life in the sex industry to finding herself in the lineage of Jesus Christ is such a beautiful picture of the way God works. His redeeming love makes old things in your life pass away, and all things in your life become new.

One of the main reasons I have used the disciplines found in the life of Boaz is that Boaz was a one-woman man. He loved Ruth like every woman wants and needs to be loved. Boaz was a foreshadow of Jesus, the one who was to come. He loved Ruth the way Jesus would love us. These are disciplines that every girl needs to know so she can watch for them and wait for them to be demonstrated in a guy's life. I pray every guy will pursue and incorporate these things in their lives as well- not because Boaz had them, but because Jesus does.

When a guy will learn and incorporate these five disciplines in his life then he can see what powerful works God can do in his relationship. A guy should look at his life now. Is he doing what he has been told to do by others, regarding relationships? If he is, how has that plan been working for him? Most importantly, does the Lord see his behavior and say 'Well done!'?"

When guys are living out these five disciplines, or at least getting in the race to develop them, so many of the perpetual complex issues of love and marriage can be resolved. Relationships will be healthy and strong, thriving and uplifting, as well as enabling and enduring when these disciplines are pursued.

A guy must decide if he wants that. Does anyone want that anymore? I think he does.

Please find a Bible- in a church, in your house, on your phone or on your computer- and read the whole book of Ruth. I think you will see why it is their story God picked to teach me these five disciplines. If you should want to know God's "whole story" for your life, not just his message in Ruth, keep reading the Bible. There is good news in the words God wrote.

THE BIBLE IS ONE BIG LOVE STORY OF GOD'S EFFORTS
TO REACH OUT TO YOU AND SHOW YOU HOW MUCH
HE LOVES YOU.

CHAPTER FOUR:
DISCUSSION QUESTIONS

1. *Why do you think Elimelech took his family to a pagan land to escape the famine?*

What other family in the Old Testament fled to a pagan land for rescue from a famine?

What do each of these stories tell us about Gods sovereignty?

2. *Read about Rahab in Joshua 2, 3:20-25.*
Write down your thoughts about Rahab, a prostitute, being the mother of Boaz.

  a. Grace

  b. Parenting

  c. Redeemed life

What do you learn from the scripture about her relationship with God?

3. What truths about God bring you hope from reading these passages in Ruth and Joshua?

32

CHAPTER FIVE:
The Fundamentals

For the remainder of the book, we are going to study 5 principles that we learn from the story of Boaz and Ruth and how they can help us honor one another in relationships. Those 5 things are: Favor, Provision, Protection, Affirmation, and Integrity.

But, before we dive into those principles in-depth, first we need to lay the groundwork by discussing some fundamental prerequisites that we'll need to understand to better implement the 5 things in our lives.

FUNDAMENTAL #1

This is a study of the life of Boaz and how he loved Ruth; however, *it is Jesus that you ultimately need to emulate.* Boaz is a picture of Jesus. So as you delve into Boaz's life and see these disciplines develop, always be aware that it is because of his love for and obedience to God that these are possible. When a girl wants to wait on someone, she might want to wait on someone like Boaz, but in doing so, who she is really waiting on is someone like Jesus, and that is always good.

FUNDAMENTAL #2

Understand and be able to define the relationship you are in. If there is not a clear understanding of how relationships are different, a guy will not know the appropriate way to demonstrate these five disciplines toward the girl in his life.

These levels of relationships are rooted in the understanding that scripture refers to different types of love that God asks to share. Throughout God's Word we see demonstrated three basic ways we love others:

Agape' - selfless, sacrificial, unconditional love.
This is the love God has for us.

Those who accept my commandments and obey them are the ones who love me. Because they love me, my Father will love them. And I will love them and reveal myself to each of them."
John 14:21

Philia - close friendship or brotherly love.
These relationships are found with family members, close friends, acquaintances, and those you spend a lot of time with.

Love each other with genuine affection, and take delight in honoring each other.
Romans 12:10

Eros- *the physical, sensual love between a husband and wife that is found in the Old Testament book Song of Solomon.*

The love you feel for the one you desire to marry; that romantic love that accompanies agape' love. Knowing how to express this love in the way God intends is imperative in order for you to have the blessings of God on such a relationship.

"Kiss me and kiss me again, for your love is sweeter than wine. How pleasing is your fragrance; your name is like the spreading fragrance of scented oils. No wonder all the young women love you! Take me with you; come, let's run! The king has brought me into his bedroom."

Song of Solomon 1:2-4 (NLT)

Knowing these different types of love will help you determine what is appropriate in how you manifest these 5 Things in the different relationships you have. For example, you should not hold

hands with or kiss your co-worker if you are dating someone else, and certainly not if you are married to someone else. You wouldn't shake hands when saying goodnight to your wife like you might do with dinner guests when they leave. I think you get the idea.

There are three basic levels of relationships based on the three types of love we find in scripture. Not to appear patronizing for the more relationship-savvy people, the reason I am even including these in the book is because over the years of counseling and teaching on relationships principles, I have learned not to assume that everyone has a clear understanding of how to define relationships. When you don't have clear definitions, you make big mistakes, and those usually result in big hurts. Here are the basics:

A.   Level 1 = friend, acquaintance, human being

You should demonstrate all 5 Things in these people's lives. Since they are a reflection of the character of Christ, everyone should be a beneficiary in their appropriate forms.

For God loved the world so much that he gave his one and only Son, so that everyone who believes in him will not perish but have eternal life..

John 3:16

B. Level 2 = someone who is closer to you than a casual acquaintance.

You might have years of friendship history, or because they are related to you (sister, mom, grandmother, children), or because you are beginning to date them or considering dating them. This level would include philia and agape' love. Biblical examples of this level of relationship would be Jesus and his mother Mary, Ruth and mother-in-law Naomi, Jesus and his disciples, Jonathan and his dear friend David, Paul and his young ministry partner Timothy, Mary and her cousin Elizabeth, and Jesus and the family of Mary, Martha, and their brother Lazarus.

C. Level 3 = only one person can fit in this category, and that will be your spouse, or the one you are dating or engaged to marry.

No one should feel the depth, commitment, and full strength of all the 5 Things more than this one person. This is all of the loves put together exclusively for this one person. You give them every kind of love: agape', philia, and eros. Even within this level, there are boundaries of purity that are required in God's plan. Sexual activity is blessed by God only in the covenant of marriage. There are other expressions of eros love that are appropriate for the one you are dating or engaged. These feelings of romantic love should never be expressed to anyone else.

THE ONLY EXCEPTION WE HAVE IN LOVING SOMEONE
MORE, ACCORDING TO SCRIPTURE, IS IN YOUR
RELATIONSHIP WITH JESUS CHRIST- WHICH SHOULD
MAKE ALL OTHER RELATIONSHIPS LOOK PALE IN
COMPARISON. HE COMMANDS US TO LOVE
ALL OTHERS (INCLUDING OUR SPOUSE)
LESS THAN WE LOVE HIM.

FUNDAMENTAL #3

Know what God's definition of love is and what it looks like. A guy or girl can't just say they love someone and not know how that is put into action. Memorize these truths and incorporate them into your life. When you learn to love like this, you will have the knowledge and thus the tools to demonstrate selfless love within all of your relationships. The following three areas of biblical truth are the plumb line God gives to measure whether you are or are not authentically loving.

A. God Is Love – The Bible teaches us that you know how to love when you know God because he is love. And the only way to know God is to know Jesus. Jesus says that when you have seen him, you have seen his Father. This makes it clear that in order to truly love someone else, you must love God first. Wait for someone who knows that God is love and loves Jesus, so they can then know how to love you.

Dear friends, let us continue to love one another, for love comes from God. Anyone who loves is a child of God and knows God. But anyone who does not love does not know God, for God is love. God showed how much he loved us by sending his one and only Son into the world so that we might have eternal life through him. This is real love-not that we loved God, but that he loved us and sent his Son as a sacrifice to take away our sins. Dear friends, since God loved us that much, we surely ought to love each other. No one has ever seen God. But if we love each other, God lives in us, and his love is brought to full expression in us."

1 John 4:7-12

B. Love is not - jealous, prideful, rude, arrogant, wanting your own way, irritable, resentful, being glad when someone is wronged (1 Corinthians 13). These are relationship killers Know them well. While it is in you to occasionally find these sins felt and demonstrated, be diligent to recognize them as sin. Call them what they are, then seek forgiveness from the one(s) you have wounded with these behaviors. Go before the Lord and ask for forgiveness, mercy, and strength to repent and not act out in the behavior again. Accountability is a great tool in strengthening this area of discipline.

C. Love is - patient with others, kind toward all people, happy when truth is known, able to bear all things you are confronted with, able to believe all things can be used of God and for God, hopeful in all things because your faith is in the one who is your hope, able to endure anything that is put in your path of life whether good or bad, and finally, love never fails. Love from God never quits working, it always accomplishes what God intended it to accomplish. (1 Corinthians 13).

"Love is patient and kind. Love is not jealous or boastful or proud or rude. It does not demand its own way. It is not irritable, and it keeps no record of being wronged. It does not rejoice about injustice but rejoices whenever the truth wins out. Love never gives up, never loses faith, is always hopeful, and endures every circumstance."

1 Corinthians 13:4-8

I encourage you to get these scriptures memorized. Anchor them in your heart and meditate on them every day and night. These are fundamental truths that are needed in order to support the five disciplines you are about to get into. This journey is going to be so much fun.

CHAPTER FIVE:
DISCUSSION QUESTIONS

1. *List some examples of relationships that are representative of each of the types of love defined in Chapter 5:*

Agape' –

Philia –

Eros –

2. *Why is it important to understand the "levels" of relationships you are in?*

What might occur if these are unclear to either person in a relationship?

3. Based on 1st Corinthians 13, write down what scripture teaches us that love is and is not, what it does, and what it does not do:

Love is: Love is not: Love does: Love does not:

*list any other attributes of Love you find in other scripture.

44

Thing #1: Favor

"Boaz went over and said to Ruth 'Listen, my daughter. Stay right here with us when you grain; don't go to any other fields. Stay right behind the young women working in my field. See which part of the field they are harvesting and then follow them. I have warned the young men not to treat you roughly. Ad when you are thirsty, help yourself to the water they have drawn from the well. Ruth fell at his feet and thanked him warmly. 'What have I done to deserve such kindness?' she asked. 'I am only a foreigner.'"

Ruth 2:8–10

After years of teaching these principles, I don't know if there is not more leverage in this particular attribute than all of the others. It is the one I continue to hear the most discussion over. This surprises me a little, but then I realize – why should it surprise me? Where would I be without the favor of the Lord? How would my heart respond when the one I love the most begins to favor another over me? With such deep, and broad emotion attached to this gift from another, is it any wonder why the word Favor is so precious and powerful and sustaining and life giving?

The word "kindness" is the taken from the same word that we get "favor" and it is a huge thing. For a guy to show a girl favor is to accept her, to choose her for something unique and special. The girl he picks is the one he favors. He will show graciousness toward her and take pleasure in her presence and he delights in her. Isn't it wonderful to think of someone delighting in you? Delight has become one of my new favorite words. It is such a remarkable gift for someone to show you favor by taking delight in you. Boaz showed Ruth favor.

Before Boaz ever noticed Ruth, he came home from a trip and greeted his workers with a blessing from God, which established right away his character and the kind of authority figure he was. When he began to look over his fields and saw Ruth for the first time, he asked his workers about her. Yes— he saw her and inquired about her.

It seems things weren't too different back then than they are now, regarding wanting to know about a girl. Boaz was just a good man who saw someone new and wanted to know who she was. How many times has a guy been at a party, an event or even at church, noticed a girl, then turned his back to her so she could not read his lips, and asked a friend, "Ok, who is the girl over there by the chair with the black dress and dark brown hair?" This is what Boaz was doing, even though he had good reason to ask about her since she was working in his field.

The desire of Ruth's heart was that someone would be gracious enough to allow her to glean the leftover barley in the fields, after the workers had harvested the heartiest stalks of wheat. She hoped someone would say it was okay for her to be there and welcome her to work there. Boaz gave her that

notes:

46

favor.

Boaz showed Ruth favor when he told her to "listen carefully" to him. He asked her to not work in any other field, but to stay and work with him. He assured her that she would have work available throughout the duration of the harvest season.

Boaz also told her he would make sure she had everything she needed. She would not lack for anything, because she was special to him and he delighted in her presence, and, he had heard of her good character in the way that she was faithful to Naomi. Oh yes, he favored her alright. Then Ruth did something that every girl needs to learn to do. She acknowledged that favor by speaking a word of gratitude.

"I hope I continue to please you sir,' she replied. 'You have comforted me by speaking so kindly to me, even though I am not one of your workers.'"

Ruth 2:13

Ruth pointed out specific ways Boaz had favored her; therefore, affirming his delight toward her. She told him how he made her feel comfortable working for him. He made her feel wanted and welcomed wherever he was. She felt special, and that came from him making her feel safe and comfortable with the crew of workers under his employ.

Girls need to say thank you more often when guys show them acts of favor. If she will start naming the specific acts of kindness, graciousness or delight shown toward her, it may encourage more acts of kindness. It's not a manipulation; it's a word of confirmation. Guys get called out quickly for their acts that girls find gross, rude and inappropriate, so start a movement that thanks guys for their acts of a noble nature, favor and kindness. Name the act specifically so he is clear on what good thing he has done.

Ruth also reminded Boaz of how he spoke kindly to her. Proverbs 18:21 tells us that words are the source of life and death in your spirit, so how much more would it be crucial to speak kind, healing words in the life of the one you are in love with? Boaz always spoke with consideration of Ruth's needs. Kind words are a healing balm. Proverbs 15:1 says words can stop anger and thus change the direction of a bad day. "Kind words are like honey-sweet to the soul and healthy for the body" Proverbs 16:24. Guys should want to be the one who causes anger, anxiousness, and fear to disappear from their favored one's life. If he shows her favor through his words, this can be accomplished.

When something great happens, don't you find that you can't wait to tell someone? Ruth was the same way. When she got through working in the fields, the first thing she did when she got home was tell Naomi, her mother-in-law, all of the wonderful things she had experienced since she met Boaz. She showed Naomi all of the leftover food that Boaz sent home with her, as well as the extra wheat she was given. She also reported how he told her to stay with his workers until the whole harvesting season was over. Naomi was so thankful and rejoiced at Ruth's good fortune and blessings.

She told Ruth to stay in this man's fields through the whole harvest season and be thankful for God's blessings! Ruth continued to work for Boaz. What a wise girl! What a great spring!

When a man loves a woman, and wants to pursue her, he must show her favor. She needs to know that she is favored above all other girls in his life, even his mom. She also needs to know that he favors her over other hobbies and interests he might have as well. Hear me clearly, it is not that he should refrain from having any other interests or hobbies. That would be tragic. But, when she knows that no other person or interests in his life take precedence over her, there is a peace and security that resides in her spirit. Favor is when a man creates within a woman a certainty that if he could only pick one person to have with him on a deserted island, he would pick her. Favor is showing her that if she really needed him at home, he would stay and help instead of golf, or hunting or any other option he might have. It's when she knows that if he was asked to pick out the prettiest girl in the room, he would point to her. It is when he chooses her idea over another's. Favor in a healthy, loving home, is a dad showing their children that he and their mother are a united team. Favor shown to a girl can rescue her heart from insecurity and discouragement and establish her feet on a path of contentment and joy.

A girl wants to be clear that she is his favorite. Always. How a guy expresses that favor toward her will look different depending on each guy's personality. Relationships can be so much more fulfilling when guys are free to express favor without being compared to another guys expression of favor to the girl he loves. One guy may prefer and delight in bringing a girl flowers and writing a poem. Another guy may show favor by asking her on a date and paying for the meal and the movie, while another may show favor by saving a girl a seat by him at some event. Another way a guy might show favor is to get a big tattoo on his arm of a heart with her name in the middle of it or have her name burned into the back of his leather belt for all to see when he wears his favorite Levi's. Don't you love it? There are as many ways to show favor as there are personalities, and that is one of the many ways that makes life and love so much fun. This leaves absolutely no room for comparison. Often, the death of a guy's desire to show any acts of favor is that he is continually compared to other guys, and thus, quenching his spirit. Let it go. Enjoy the expression of his unique personality and how that will impact the way he shows you his favor.

The underlying principle of favor should always be clear in its expression—that he has made her his favorite, and he delights in showing her that. A girl's willingness to trust a guy with her life, her future, and her heart puts her in a very vulnerable place, so exercising the discipline of favor makes her feel stronger and more secure. She is peaceful and free of fear and anxiety because she is sure that his favor towards her exceeds all things except his relationship with Jesus Christ.

A word of encouragement to those guys who are fathers or hope to be a father one day. A father's favor toward his daughter is such a cornerstone in her future happiness. A little girl needs to hear her dad tell her how special she is to him. She needs to believe that he thinks she is great, regardless of academic achievement, athletic performances or social status among her peers. The favor a father shows his daughter sets a standard of how she should always be treated in word and deed. When a girl has never experienced favor from her father, she will continue searching for it, and by not really knowing what it is she is needing, may go from one failed relationship to another trying to find that favor that eludes her. If a girl has had an absent or disengaged father, her heart and spirit may not have felt the

power of favor and the grace and delight it is designed to bring to her life. Not only is it crippling for girls who have not received favor, but it handicaps young men as well. How will they know how to show favor to anyone when they have not ever seen it modeled by their fathers, or other male authorities in their lives?

Praise God that his grace can fill the void when favor has been absent from the earthly home. God favors you so much! You may have gone through several painful relationships before you realized and understood that favor is good and it comes straight from the heart of God. God has designed girls to need favor, just as He has designed guys to need to give it. Be empowered by the fact that all are created in God's image and God has shown the ultimate favor by making people the object of his affection and delight.

"As God's partners, we beg you not to accept this marvelous gift of God's kindness and then ignore it. For God says, 'At just the right time, I heard you. On the day of salvation, I helped you.' Indeed, the "right time" is now.

Today is the day of salvation."

2nd Corinthians 6:1–2

A girl needs to be grounded in the truth that complete favor will only come from her Heavenly Father, and she needs to be confident that he is enough. Her hope should always be in Christ and since marriage is to be a picture of that same hope, favor must be demonstrated in lavish and loving ways from her boyfriend so that she will trust him to show her favor as her husband as well.

For a guy to develop the discipline of favor he must be in the process of growing in Christ and learning to let go of the habits and patterns that rob him of being able to show favor, like pornography addiction, self-serving personality traits, arrogance and pride. Until he understands the favor of God, it will be harder for him to show it to others. Maturing in this discipline needs to include some other spiritual disciplines in his life that will enable the Holy Spirit to strengthen him: like Bible study, consistent prayer life, and having an older man of God mentor him and help him grow. Find a mentor who is authentic and real in his favor of others, especially the women in his family and particularly his wife, if he is married.

Girls can know if a guy will show them favor. Watch how he shows favor to the female friends and family members in his life. Are his friends and family members all treated with respect and grace? Are they recipients of kind words? Wait for a guy who is already demonstrating this discipline in his life. Anyone can make a girl feel special for a season, but the guy she needs to marry should be committed to making her feel favored over all else for a lifetime. One of the best ways a girl can have this confidence is seeing him demonstrate it toward her from the beginning of their relationship.

Guys need to consider the levels of relationships we have discussed earlier. In light of these definitions, it must be clear that the general favor shown to other girls in his life is different than the favor shown toward the girl that he is pursuing or dating. It takes a spiritually mature guy to show appropriate kindness, comfort, respect, and gentleness to all people; and yet also show the girl you have fallen in love with that she is your priority, your most favored one.

For the guys that feel ill-equipped to show favor, there is hope for you. Just read and learn in these particular stories how favor from Jesus Christ changed the lives of these individuals he encountered while here on earth.

Jesus was so gracious to Zaccheus. Here was a man hated by all because of his unscrupulous ways as a tax collector. Tax collecting in that day was characterized by cheating and stealing from those that had no recourse. When Jesus came to his town, Zaccheus climbed up in a tree because he was too short to see over the crowd already lined up to see Jesus walk by. When Jesus got to where Zacchaeus was, he looked up at him,

notes:

53

called him by name and then invited himself to dinner with Zacchaeus. Oh, the favor Zacchaeus must have felt. For the Messiah to call him by name and want to come eat at his house, when it is quite possible that no one else could even stand to be around him, must have been like a fresh wind of hope blowing into his soul. The favor Jesus showed Zacchaeus evoked a response – and what a response it was.

> *"When Jesus came by he looked up at Zacchaeus and*
> *called him by name, 'Zacchaeus!' he said. 'Quick, come down!*
> *I must be a guest in your home today.' Zacchaeus quickly climbed down and*
> *took Jesus to his house in great excitement and joy. But the people were displeased.*
> *'He has gone to be the guest of a notorious sinner.' They grumbled. Meanwhile,*
> *Zacchaeus stood before the Lord and said 'I will give half my wealth to the poor,*
> *Lord, and if I have cheated people on their taxes, I will give them back four times*
> *as much!' Jesus responded, 'Salvation has come to this home today, for this man*
> *has shown himself to be a true son of Abraham. For the Son of Man*
> *came to seek and save those who are lost."*

Luke 19:5–10

Another example is when a woman was caught in the very act of having sex with a married man and was brought out by the religious elite to the center court of the temple where Jesus was talking with a group of people. Those religious elites knew that the law said she must be stoned, so her accusers were curious to see how Jesus would handle this breach of the law. They threw her to the ground in front of Jesus and asked him what he was going to do about this woman caught in sin. I wish I knew what Jesus began to write in the sand that day and if it was those writings that provoked their responses. However, after he finished his first writing on the ground, his profound statement to them was clearly a game changer.

"...but Jesus stooped down and wrote in the dust with his finger. They kept demanding an answer, so he stood up again and said, 'All right, but let the one who has never sinned throw the first stone!' Then he stooped down again and wrote in the dust. When the accusers heard this, they slipped away one by one, beginning with the oldest, until only Jesus was left in the middle of the crowd with the woman. Then Jesus stood up again and said to the woman, 'Where are your accusers? Didn't even one of them condemn you?' 'No, Lord,' she said. And Jesus said, 'Neither do I. Go and sin no more.'"

John 8:6b–11

This story grips my soul every time I read it. To be sure, she was a sinner and guilty of the crime she was accused of, but Jesus' favor brought her deliverance when the accusers wanted destruction. When the favor of Jesus collides with your sin, it brings deliverance from your sin and not your destruction. How can we ever fully grasp the favor of forgiveness of sin? I'm not sure we can, but I am so thankful Jesus offers it to everyone. Especially me.

notes:

Another man that would never forget the favor of God was a man Jesus and his disciples met that had been born blind. Jesus' disciples asked him whose sin had caused the man's blindness—his mother's or his father's? Jesus said that no one's sin had caused the blindness, but that the man was born blind for the purpose of God having an opportunity to demonstrate his power.

"'It was not because of his sin or his parents' sins,' Jesus answered. 'This happened so the power of God could be seen I him. We must quickly carry out the tasks assigned us by the one who sent us. The night is coming, and then no one can work. But, while I am here in the world, I am the light of the world.' Then he spit on the ground, made mud with the saliva, and spread the mud over the blind man's eyes. He told him, 'Go wash yourself in the pool of Siloam' (Siloam means "sent"). So the man went and washed and came back seeing!"

John 9:3–7

The favor of Jesus can heal when the whole world says it can never happen. A man born blind had his sight restored because Jesus found him and showed him favor by giving him sight for the first time in his life. Favor brings hope to the hopeless.

There are so many more people that saw, first hand, the favor of God: Abraham, Esther, the woman at the well in Samaria, Lazarus, Mary Magdalene and countless others. He told them all in word or deed that he took pleasure in loving them. He wanted them to know and wants you to know, that you are favored by him. He delights in you and has made a way for you to know him. He desires to have fellowship with you because you are loved and therefore favored.

"They replied, "Believe in the Lord Jesus, and you will be saved,
along with everyone in your household."

Acts 16:31

Even a guy's best demonstrations of favor pale in the shadow of the Redeemer and his choosing to bring grace, healing, hope, forgiveness and salvation to a people that were lost. Praise God for the favor of his son! Praise God that Jesus modeled for everyone a perfect example of favor. And praise God that every guy has available to him the resources to show favor and it not be left up to his own abilities and experience.

"The Lord approves of those who are good,
but he condemns those who plan wickedness."

Proverbs 12:2

"The man who finds a wife finds a treasure, and he receives favor from the Lord."

Proverbs 18:22

CHAPTER SIX:
DISCUSSION QUESTIONS

Introduction Exercise - Write down 10 qualities you value most in the person you would date:

1.	6.
2.	7.
3.	8.
4.	9.
5.	10.

Now go back over your list and circle the attributes that are BIBLICAL. How would you describe, based on your list, what you value?

1. *What does the bible tell us about these 3 people in the book of Ruth? What is their background?*

Naomi –

Ruth –

Boaz –

2. *Define FAVOR:*

3. *List the verses in Ruth where you see Boaz showing FAVOR:*

4. *Find at least 3 other Bible verses, other than the ones mentioned in the "5 Things" verses that demonstrate how God showed his FAVOR to someone AND how he shows His FAVOR toward us:*

1.

2.

3.

5. *How can guys show appropriate FAVOR to girls before they are engaged or married?*

List 4 practical ways:

1.
2.
3.
4.

6. *This week's observation- How did you observe guys showing FAVOR to girls this week? Record these observations*

*GIRLS * Remember to say "thank you!", and be specific, when you observe this kindness being shown.*

1.
2.
3.

60

Thing #2: Provision

"…And when you are thirsty,

help yourself to the water they have drawn from the well." Ruth 2:9b

"So Ruth worked alongside the women in Boaz's fields and gathered grain with them until the end of the barley harvest. Then she continued working with them through the wheat harvest in early summer. And all the while she lived with her mother-in-law." Ruth 2:23

"When Ruth went back to work again, Boaz ordered his young men, 'Let her gather grain right among the sheaves without stopping her. And pull out some heads of barley from the bundles and drop them on purpose for her. Let her pick them up, and don't give her a hard time!" Ruth 2:15-16

"Now don't worry about a thing, my daughter. I will do what is necessary…"
Ruth 3:11a

"Then Boaz said to her, 'Bring your cloak and spread it out.' He measure six scoops of barley into the cloak and placed it on her back. Then he returned to the town. When Ruth went back to her mother-in-law, Naomi asked, 'What happened, my daughter?' Ruth told Naomi everything Boaz had done for her, and she added, 'He gave me these six scoops of barley and said, 'Don't go back to your mother-in-law empty handed.''' Ruth 3:15-17

The second discipline every guy needs to demonstrate and every girl needs to wait for is provision - the basic ability and desire to provide for the needs of the ones you love: family, friends, and the girl you love. Boaz provided the needs of Ruth, her mother-in-law, and others employed by him. He was a giver of what he had worked for and earned.

There are two particular ways that we saw Boaz provide for Ruth.

PUBLIC PROVISION

Public provisions his open, public demonstration of provision for those he loved. First, he provided her a job. Though she had been hired by his overseers before he arrived at the fields, he allowed her not only to stay for that season, but provided her a place to glean throughout both of the harvest seasons. Ruth would typically be left to father the little that was available after the harvesters has gone over the filled and definitely not assured of a job during the next harvest. But, Boaz assured her of both - stay here for the remainder of this season and come back for the next one as well. What a generous provision he made for her.

Ruth was also provided for in a public way when he invited her to eat with the harvesters at lunch and made sure she had all she wanted. He sent leftovers home with Ruth for Naomi and her, as well as sending some home with those working in his fields.

Provision involves giving from what you have. Generosity with what For has provided for you is a way to say thank you to the Lord as well as to bring glory to him.

"Let your light shine before men in such a way that they may see your good works, and glorify your Father who is in heaven."
Matthew 5:16 (NASB).

Public provision is a way in which a guy demonstrates to others how much he loves the girl that he favors. Appropriate public displays of provision are just showing love to someone by providing for what they need.

A few years ago I was teaching these principles at a retreat for junior high and high school girls. Teaching these disciplines to high school girls was fun and fairly easy because they are at an age where it is not a huge leap to make the connection between their stage of life and thinking about the guy they want to marry. They are thinking about marriage already. However, I was worried a little bit about making the transfer of these principles to those girls that were in junior high. Some of them were twelve years old, and hopefully not thinking too much about who they were going to marry. But, the truth is I wanted it to work because it would be an opportunity to be preventive of many of the traps the world has waiting for them when they do being to date. If they could understand what these disciplines mean and how they might be appropriately demonstrated by guys at their age, then they would be much more equipped to make good decisions in the future.

When the junior high girls came to my session I began to explain each of these five disciplines that they needed to look for and appreciate in their guy friends. When I got to provision, I asked them if they could give me some examples of how a young guy their age might provide for them in an age appropriate way. Immediately one young girl, a sixth grader, said, "Well, the other day I was on my way to my locker and dropped all of my books in the hallway. Then Blake Jones ran over to me and started picking them up for me and offered to carry them to my locker for me." I cheered and told her that was exactly what I was talking about. I asked her if she thanked him for helping her, and she said she had. At that time another young girl, another sixth grader, added that she remembered a time when it was pouring down rain and she has gotten her clothes wet and began telling her fiends that she was cold. This same 'Blake Jones' came and offered his jacket to her saying he didn't really want to wear it anyway, and she was welcome to borrow it for the rest of the day. Immediately I asked them who in the world was 'Blake Jones' and to tell me who his parents are so I can call them and give them some kind of parenting award!

What I learned that day is that God does indeed put it in our hearts to need things and to want to provide things. You don't have to be an adult to "get it". This young man clearly had this discipline modeled for him by someone in his life and he was just doing what he had learned was the right thing - to provide for someone who has a need if you have the resources to meet that need. Well done, 'Blake Jones,' and well done sixth grade girls for recognizing greatness. (Blake Jones is not his real name of course).

Private Provision

In my opinion, one of the most romantic scenes in Ruth was when Boaz instructed his workers to pull some of the best stalks of grain from their bundles and leave them on the ground for Ruth to pick up during her gleaning time. He provided his very best for her! Ruth was so favored. Without Ruth knowing, he graciously made sure she had access to more than just what would be left over. In doing this Boaz made it clear to those working for him that Ruth was indeed highly favored. While this was a private provision for Ruth in that she did not know this scheme had been formed, it was a public provision witnessed by others.

There have been many conversations about the purpose of private provision and why that might have been Boaz's course of action. Some of the thoughts expressed were that it was possibly a way to help Ruth not feel obligated in any way to repay him, or maybe he knew the potential for jealousy and division due to him showing Ruth favor among the workers and so he didn't want to put her in a precarious and dangerous situation.

Private provision can eliminate conflict with others. Boaz's provision for Ruth seemed to be born out of his genuine care for her. His faithfulness to God provide a desire to meet the needs of people, and because he favored Ruth, maybe Boaz just delighted in seeing her joy after receiving the blessing of the extra. So a few good reasons to provide privately: eliminate conflict among the group a girl is in, prevent jealousy which can impact her life in a negative way, avoid a perceived need to repay and therefore circumvent the "I owe him something" mindset, and because often it brings a guy joy to provide for her needs without getting the glory, but only to see the surprise and happiness it brings to her life.

When a guy finds joy in providing needs and wants in others' lives, he finds that his capacity to show favor through provision is more than he ever dreamed. To provide great of small things for the one he loves, just because he can, is actually an act of gratitude to the Lord. I have seen and head testimonies of guys leaving a sweet note of a girl's windshield, or he secretly payed her rent. One guy brought home dinner and has her apartment clean when she got home from work. Other guys have made arrangements to have flowers waiting on her desk at work, or put extra money in her purse before a trip. One of the most generous acts of provision was when one guy gave his girlfriend all of his french fries just because he knew she loved them.

When guys are learning bow to implement these disciplines, it is often best to start practicing with the girls that are friends in their life right now. A guy can help if her car is in need of repair, and she needs a ride somewhere. She might need help with a class she is taking or in an academic subject he excels in. Provision is not just about paying for something.

In order to prevent any misunderstanding between the guys and girls in why these acts of provision are being made, there have been guys that worked in groups who have washed cars, left encoring notes and then all of the guys signed the card saying it was from all of them. Groups of guys have brought dinner for several of their female friends and let them have a 'girl's night out.' They delighted in making provision, but didn't want anyone to think there was some hidden agenda behind their efforts. This should resonate in every guy's spirit when it is done because he is created and designed to provide, not because Boaz did, but because God did it first.

Boaz also provided privately for Ruth and Naomi when Ruth went to the barn where Boaz was working to let him know she was willing to marry him, which was done in a way that was customary in those times and culture, (more about this later). Boaz provided a coat full of barley for her to take home for Naomi and herself. This was a private showing of love and provision and thus favor towards Ruth. When she got home and Naomi asked what Boaz said to her she reported that he said, "these six measures of barley he gave me, for he said, 'Do not go to your mother-in-law empty handed'" (Ruth 3:16-17).

Can you imagine how this profoundly impacted Ruth's heart since she was the sole caregiver of her mother-in-law? When a guy truly loves a girl, he must be willing to provide for who she must provide for as well when they get married. If she is a widow or a single mom, he wants to help provide for her children. If she has a sick parent, he wants to help ease the burden of her responsibility. Should she have a sister or brother unable to care for themselves or who has fallen on hard times, this just provides another way for him to love her through providing help for those in her life.

A GUY JUST GIVES, HELPS AND PROVIDES BECAUSE HE CAN, AND HE CAN BECAUSE GOD GAVE ALL HE HAD TO HELP AND PROVIDE FOR HIM.

"And this same God who takes care of me will supply all your needs from his glorious riches, which have been given to us in Christ Jesus."

Philippians 4:19

"Once I was young, and now I am old. Yet I have never seen the godly abandoned or their children begging for bread."

Psalm 37:25

CHAPTER SEVEN:
DISCUSSION QUESTIONS

1. *We talked about Philippians 4:19 in our Bible study. Fill in the blanks –*
"And my _____ will supply _____ your _____
according to _____ riches in glory in _____
_____."

2. *Find 3 more ways in the Bible where God PROVIDES for someone.*
        *BONUS points for finding where He provided "privately".

3. *How do you think PROVISION reflects God's character?*

4. *List at least 4 ways you are PROVIDED for this week*

       1.   3.

       2.   4.

5. GUYS: List 3 ways you PROVIDED help in some way for a girl this week.

GIRLS: List 3 ways a guy PROVIDED for a need you had and you thanked them.

   1.

   2.

   3.

72

CHAPTER EIGHT:
Thing #3: Protection

"I have warned the young men not to treat you roughly."

Ruth 2:9

"When Ruth went back to work again, Boaz ordered his young me, 'Let her gather grain right among the sheaves without stopping her. And pull out some heads of barley from the bundles and drop them on purpose for her. Let her pick them up and don't give her a hard time!'"

Ruth 2:15-16

"So Ruth lay at Boaz's feet until the morning, but she got up before it was light enough for people to recognize each other. For Boaz had said, 'No one must know that a woman was here at the threshing floor.'

Ruth 3:14

Guys are designed by God to protect. Boaz demonstrated for us how far reaching the discipline of protection can be. This protection is a discipline that the Holy Spirit of God develops in a guy in order to manifest the image of God in which he was created.

Protection is especially crucial in the life of the girl a guy is committing his life to in marriage. The consequences of a girl left feeling unsafe, in any area of her life, can have crippling effects. In the story of Boaz and Ruth, we learn three particular area of Ruth's life in which he protected her.

1. Boaz protected her body- he commanded the men working for him not to touch her. Ruth, being a widow, and a laborer, as well as a foreigner in his fields, was an easy target and very vulnerable to the unscrupulous ways of men around her. Although it's hard to imagine that any of the women would be susceptible to evil and perverted behavior from men while employed by a man such as Boaz, he still made sure Ruth was shielded from any inappropriate advances or harm. It is significant that he not only commanded his male workers not to touch her, but he told Ruth that he had secured her protection as well. She was, therefore, able to work with peace and confidence that no one would bring her harm.

A guy who loves, and thus protects, never hits a girl. He walks on the "street side", he holds her arm or hand when in a crowd to keep her safely close to him. A guy who protects will walk ahead and guide her when in a tense or dangerous situation. A guy's need to protect compels him to rush to her is her car is broken down or wrecked to ensure she is safe. A protector will stand between a mom and a rebellious child who is threatening bodily harm. He will answer the knock on the door when it is late at night in order to protect his family. He might even go to war to ensure she will live in safety and free from those who might threaten that peace. These noble protectors will take bullets, stop criminals, run into burning buildings, climb mountains, run into hurricanes and dive into the swelling tides to save people he loves - even to save someone he doesn't know. He is designed by God to protect. That's how he loves.

Another way guys can protect their favored one physically, is by not being promiscuous. This is not done just for her physical protection, but because that is what God requires, and doing so is an act of obedience. The Bible is clear that "Marriage is to be held in honor among all, and the marriage bed is to be undefiled; for fornicators and adulterers God will judge." Hebrews 13:4 (NASB). Having multiple sexual partners does not protect the physical health of a guy's future wife. On the contrary, it clearly put her at great risk of contracting sexually transmitted diseases.

A guy also protects by not having sex with his girlfriend before he is married to her. If a guy is going to be a protector, he must start with protecting a girl from the lust of his own flesh. He should not tempt her to compromise her obedience to the commands of God's word to keep herself pure. The Bible says *"Flee from sexual immorality. All other sins a person commits are outside the body, but whoever sins sexually, sins against their own body."* I Corinthians 6:18 (NIV)

If the command for sexual purity has already been violated, the great news is that God can redeem the sin against the body. God's forgiveness is made possible by the blood shed on the cross. There is hope for a great future if one repents and beings to walk in the life of faithfulness and obedience. God's Word promises that "If we confess our sins, he is faithful and just and will forgive us our sins and purify us from all unrighteousness" (1 John 1:9, NIV)

One of the most profound examples I have heard regarding the impact of protection came from a speaker at a human trafficking conference. The speaker was the director of ministry that helps the homeless as well as rescues women being trafficked. She told of a time when she and her husband were called in to the police station one night to help a woman who had been taken off the street. She was trembling and shaking with fear because of the threats that were made against her by her pimp. They decided to take her with them in order to ensure her safety. After they placed her in the backseat of their car, they began to drive around while deciding where she should stay for the night. Cassie shared how this young woman was so anxious, fearful, and frantically looking around to see if anyone was following them. Hearing her cries and seeing her anxious behavior, her husband stopped the car and turned around to face her. With great resolve and gentleness, he looked straight in her eyes and told her that

she need not be afraid anymore. He assured her that those men could not hurt her now. If they tried, they would have to go through him first to get to her, and that wasn't going to happen. The confirmation of the impact of this discipline came when the speaker told the crowd that she had never been more attracted to her husband than in that moment, watching him vow to protect a vulnerable and scared young woman. This is how a guy can speak transforming words and perform life-changing acts of protection when he is empowered by the indwelling Holy Spirit of God.

While guys are powerful protectors, girls have been in the position of needing to protect as well. Many times she has done it with selfless passion and supernatural strength. Several stories in the Bible illustrate this amazing ability of girls to protect.

Genesis 16 tells how Hagar, after being kicked out of the camp she was living in, protected her baby son, Ishmael, from the desert prey, believing her son would surely die. She was waving away animals and vultures and placing her body over him in order to keep the blazing sun from parching his little body. A mother's protection is fierce. God saved him from harm and enabled them to get to safety.

1 Samuel, chapter 25 tells how Abigail's husband, Nabal, refused to help King David with some of the needed supplies for his soldiers. This refusal incurred the wrath of the king. Nabal's inability to protect his family came as a result of his perpetual drunkenness. Abigail's wise, humble, yet bold intervention on behalf of her family before the king and his soldiers spared her family and all of their land from the imminent destruction.

When a law was enacted with the explicit purpose of persecuting and killing the Jews who lived in the country, Queen Esther decided she would risk death in order to save her people. In the book named after her, scripture suggests that God had possibly brought her to this important position for "just such a time as this." Esther was fearless in her desire to protect her people by approaching her husband, the king, without being summoned, which was against the law. Esther spoke to him on behalf of her people and opposed the new edict that would put her people in peril. Because he valued and honored Esther, the king changed the law to protect her people.

In the second chapter of Exodus, Jochabed, mother of Moses, protected him from the death threats of Pharaoh by creating a waterproof basket for Moses to float in down the river as a way of escape. Jochabed had Moses's sister, Miriam, follow and watch as the little basket floated down the river so she could protect him, if needed, as well as see what happened to him. Ironically, Pharaoh's own daughter saw the basket floating by and rescued him.

There is a common thread here. People who were loved were fiercely and courageously protected. So carry on, woman of God! Protection of those she loves is a manifestation of the image of God in her life. All of these people were protected because a holy God intervened.

2. Boaz protected her spirit. Remember how Boaz, in his provision for Ruth, asked his workers to drop some of the best stalks of grain on the ground for her on purpose without her knowing it? He also commanded them to not embarrass or humiliate her when she would being to pick up these talks that were clearly not the remnants she was supposed to gather. He saw the potential for her to be humiliated and made sure to protect her spirit. What an ugly scene it would have been had they started yelling out to her and fussing at her for picking up portions of grain she had no right to gather. Boaz was thinking about her spirit and wanted to protect it from being wounded. When a guy has a favored one, she should be protected from being embarrassed, ridiculed, or demeaned by anyone, especially her protector. It is a guy's obligation to see that no one brings harm to her spirit when it is within his power.

The human spirit is a powerful, yet vulnerable part of every person. The book of wisdom teaches, "A cheerful heart is good medicine, but a broken spirit saps a person's strength." Proverbs 17:22

When there is someone he loves, he will want to protect the place in a girl's life that holds hope, faith, and love - which is her spirit.

The Holy Spirit indwelling us is the greatest power a person can have. His presence enables one to endure, overcome, and thrive when there has been someone who wounded their spirit. In my twenty-five years of ministry to college students, as well as women and youth, I have heard testimony after testimony that bears witness to the fact that a broken spirit is one of the most debilitating conditions of life. It seems to be just as hard to overcome a broken spirit as any physical abuse they may have endured at the hands of boyfriends, fathers, or other relatives.

"He heals the brokenhearted and bandages their wounds. He counts the stars and calls them all by name. How great is our Lord! His power is absolute! His understanding is beyond comprehension!"

Psalm 147:3-5

Girls - wait for the guy who protects your spirit. If he is the source of criticism, ridicule, or sarcasm either privately, or in front of others, I implore you to reconsider your relationship with him. There are guys who want to be like Christ. They long to love someone by using words of kindness and they want to speak words of strength and encouragement into your spirit. Look for this guy; wait for him. I know these guys are out there, because I have met many of them and they are waiting for you, too!

3. Boaz protected her character.   According to Jewish custom at the time, Ruth would present herself to Boaz in such a manner as to let him know she was willing to marry him. It was late at night when she went to see him, and he had already fallen asleep. When he discovered her there, Ruth let her intentions be known, and they discussed their future together. It was still dark when they finished their talk, but in the early morning hours. Boaz knew that he must protect Ruth's character from unfounded rumors about any appearance of immoral behavior. Before she left he instructed the workers not to tell anyone that she has been there and to help her get out of the barn without anyone seeing her. Boaz took this action not to hide something she had done wrong, but to protect her character from assault in spite of what she had done right.

One way guys must protect girls is to stop engaging in inappropriate and vulgar conversations about girls. Rebuke the ungodly conversations that compromise the reputation of girls, as well as the character destruction that can come from the lips of other guys. God forbid these conversations come from the lips of guys who proclaim the name of Christ.

"May the words of my mouth and the meditations of my heart, be pleasing to you."

Psalm 19:14

It is time for guys to repent before the Lord and find victory over this sinful behavior. As a defender of her character, a guy can be the wall of protection around a girl when conversations around him become toxic, demeaning, and harmful to her reputation. Be bold, be vigilant. And, may every single guy choose his words with salt by speaking up and putting an end to the conversations that may damage, compromise, or even ruin the character of one of the girls God designed him to protect.

Isn't it interesting that man's first job in the garden was to protect and look after all living things that were placed there? It was a safe place for all living things. If a girl is protected, then there is no fear for her to dream and to enjoy the journey of life God has created for her. Her protection is fundamentally in the hands of an all-powerful God, but knowing that her husband is going to protect her gives her tremendous additional peace.

Jesus protected a woman caught in adultery in John 8:1-11. Even though she was guilty of sin, Jesus stood between her and the mob. When he called them out on their own sin, the accusers and onlookers all walked away. Only one man was left standing by her after the crowd left that day - Jesus. It is a powerful truth that the only one left standing there was the only one who could forgive her, restore her, and love her like no other. That agape love is so perfect and so unconditional, it should bring deep and profound hope that the ultimate protector is Jesus. He protected her body from being stoned to death. He protected her spirit when he asked, "Where are your accusers?" and she replied, "There are none here, sir" and he proclaimed, "Then neither do I accuse. Now, go on home and stop sinning." He also protected her character by literally standing up for herm causing the mob to realize they were sinners as well. He became the great equalizer and saved her character. What a gracious and merciful protector God is!

No matter what sinful acts, moral failures, or personal disgrace someone has brought on themselves - it is great to be reminded that the Savior is a protector. He will never "leave you or forsake you", but will guide and instruct in repentance and restoration. He takes lives out of the crippling mud pit and puts them securely on solid ground. Praise God!

"He lifted me out of the pit of despair, out of the mud and the mire. He set my feet on solid ground and steadied me as I walked along!"

Psalm 40:2

Pray that every guy will find that obedience to this discipline of protection will strengthen his spirit, his resolve, and his desire to protect the body, the spirit, and the character of the girl he loves. If a guy has failed to do this, then repentance and asking forgiveness is a first step in his getting back in right relationship with the Lord then obeying what God has commanded him to do. Then he can begin the journey of restoring trust and security.

GIRLS NEED A GUY'S PROTECTION, AND HIS LOVE FOR HER
IS DEMONSTRATED IN HOW HE PROTECTS HER.

CHAPTER EIGHT:
DISCUSSION QUESTIONS

1. *What goes through your mind when you think about 1 Corinthians 13:7 "Love always protects."*

What ways would you see that in action among your friends?

Where in scripture do you see God's protection of his people?

2. *(Guys) List practical ways that you can protect a girl in each of the following areas right now in your life:*

(Girls) List some specific ways that you believe guys can protect you in the 3 areas discussed in this chapter:

A. *Body –*

B. *Spirit –*

C.   Reputation –

3. (Guys) Be observant this week regarding the important role of PROTEC-TION. Record ways you were able to PROTECT girls this week.

(Girls) Be observant this week regarding the important role of PROTEC-TION. Record all the ways you saw, or heard, guys protect girls in any of the primary areas listed this week.

Thing #4: Affirmation

"Boaz replied, 'But I also know about everything you have done for your mother in law since the death of your husband. I have heard how you left your father and mother and your own land to live here among complete strangers. May the Lord, the God of Israel, under whose wings you have come to take refuge, reward you fully for what you have done.' "

Ruth 2:11-12

"'The Lord bless you, my daughter!' Boaz exclaimed. 'You are showing even more family loyalty now than you did before, for you have not gone after a younger man, whether rich or poor. Now don't worry about a thing my daughter. I will do what is necessary, for everyone in town knows you are a virtuous woman.'"

Ruth 3:10-11

Affirmation, according to the Merriam Webster dictionary means to say that something is true in a confident way, to show a strong belief in or dedication to.

The apostle Paul has a word that he wants us to always speak with confidence, *"This is a trustworthy saying, and I want you to insist on these teachings so that all who trust in God will devote themselves to doing good. These teachings are good and beneficial for everyone"* Titus 3:8

The 4th thing guys can learn from Boaz, is affirmation. Affirmations come when he speaks in confident agreement that a thing is true, regarding something he has seen in someone else's life. It is a statement of support for whatever someone is doing or saying. Affirmation also involves the discipline of listening and observing so he can find those behaviors or attributes in which he can affirm.

Boaz affirms Ruth in several areas of her life.

1. Boaz affirms Ruth's ministry and service. When Boaz first saw Ruth, he asked his workers about her. The report they gave him was about her care and love for Naomi, her mother-in-law. They told him about her willingness to move from the land of her people in Moab, and all that was familiar to her there, to Bethlehem so she could care Naomi Not only did the workers affirm Ruth when they gave such a good report, but Boaz affirmed Ruth when he shared those gracious comments with her personally. Therefore, affirming her ministry and her service before God.

This affirmation could also secure Ruth's desire to continue her ministry and service to the Lord. That is the power of affirmation.

Affirmation is a blessing and encouragement that helps keep one living life with their eyes focused on the eternal things of God, especially when life gets difficult and challenging. The power of affirmation in ministry and what is done to serve others can spur on more service. However, it not the need for affirmation that one must have in order to obey the command of Christ and serve as he has commanded, but because the pleasure of God is enough is enough.

2. Boaz affirmed Ruth's sacrificial love for Naomi. Not only did Ruth move back to Bethlehem with Naomi, but her tireless, valiant efforts to provide food for Naomi and herself were well noted and affirmed.

3. Boaz affirmed Ruth's faith by commenting on the fact that she had taken refuge under the wings of the one true God. He was encouraged by their mutual faith. Dependence on God for all of her needs was also affirmed in Ruth's life.

When Ruth vowed to Naomi that Naomi's God would be her God and that she would serve him also, we learn that Ruth's faith was in Jehovah God. Boaz saw this faith lived out in her life, so he affirmed her by speaking to her about how he had witnessed her faith to be real and authentic. Affirmations that confirm your faith walk help you 'do this by keeping our eyes on Jesus, the champion who initiates and perfects your faith." Hebrews 12:2

4. Boaz affirmed Ruth's integrity and graciousness. He affirmed her decision to choose him as her husband. Boaz knew she could have chosen someone younger and either richer or poorer than he was. He knew that she chose beyond what her eyes could see, and chose to do what God had led her to do. He affirmed Ruth by blessing her for her integrity, graciousness and kindness.

Jesus affirms people as well. It is amazing that the King of Kings, the Savior of the world, the perfect, spotless Lamb of God can find attributes in his people that he too takes notice of and affirms. What a great mystery – this presence of God and how he knows all, and sees all, and is everywhere all the time. It is hard to grasp that he can see one act of kindness or one sacrificial act expressed by one person. But, he does –

"When Jesus returned to Capernaum, a Roman officer came and pleaded with him, 'Lord, my young servant lies in bed, paralyzed and in terrible pain.' Jesus said, 'I will come and heal him.' But the officer said, 'Lord, I am not worthy to have you come into my home. Just say the word from where you are, and my servant will be healed. I know this because I am under the authority of my superior officers, and I have authority over my soldiers. I only need to say 'Go,' and they go, or 'Come,' and they come. And if I say to my slaves, 'Do this,' they do it.
When Jesus heard this, he was amazed. Turning to those who were following him, he said, 'I tell you the truth, I haven't seen faith like this in all Israel!'

Matthew 8:5-10

Jesus affirmed the faith of a woman who believed if she could just touch the hem of his coat, she would be healed.

"Just then a woman who had suffered for twelve years with constant bleeding came up behind him. She touched the fringe of his robe, for she thought, 'If I can just touch his robe, I will be healed.' Jesus turned around, and when he saw her he said, 'Daughter, be encouraged! Your faith has made you well.' And the woman was healed at that moment."

Matthew 9:20-22

Jesus asked the disciples who people thought he was. Then he asked then who they thought he was. Simon Peter replied that he believed Jesus was the Christ, the Son of the living God. Jesus affirmed Peter's proclamation by blessing him with a great responsibility.

"Jesus replied, 'You are blessed Simon son of John, because my Father in heaven has revealed this to you. You did not learn this from any human being. Now I say to you that your Peter (which means 'rock'), and upon this rock I will build my church, and all the powers of hell will not conquer it. And I will give you the keys of the Kingdom of Heaven. Whatever you forbid on earth will be forbidden I heaven, and whatever you permit on earth will be permitted in heaven,"

Matthew 16:17-19

He affirmed his love for children and their simple faith by proclaiming that anyone who receives a child in his name, receives him.

"He sat down, called the twelve disciples over to him, and said, 'Whoever wants to be first must take last place and be the servant of everyone else.' Then he put a little child among them. Taking the child in his arms, he said to them, 'Anyone who welcomes a little child like this on my behalf welcomes me, and anyone who welcomes me welcomes not only me but also my Father who sent me.'"

Matthew 16:17-19

When Jesus went to visit his friends Mar, Martha and Lazarus, Mary wanted to sit in the room and just talk to Jesus and hear what all he had to say. Martha was concerned with making sure the dinner was ready and that the preparation were in order for everyone to eat. Jesus affirmed Mary for choosing to visit with him instead of tending to other things in the house, like her sister Martha, by telling her she had chosen the best thing.

"As Jesus and the disciples continued on their way to Jerusalem, they came to a certain village where a woman named Martha welcomed him into her home. Her sister Mary, sat at the Lord's feet, listening to what he taught. But Martha was distracted by the big dinner she was preparing. She came to Jesus and said, 'Lord, doesn't it seem unfair to you that my sister just sits here while I do all the work? Tell her to come and help me.' But the Lord said to her, 'My dear Martha, you are worried and upset over all these details! There is only one thing worth being concerned about. Mary has discovered it, and it will not be taken away from her.'"

Luke 10:42

It is clear, Jesus Christ, the Savior and Redeemer, taught how to affirm by affirming others himself! He does notice, and he is delighted, when he sees his children choosing what brings him glory and honor. Rejoice in the affirmations of the Lord!

So how does a guy affirm his favored one – the one he truly loves? He would make statements of fact regarding her character, just like Boaz did and just like Jesus does. A guy who affirms will tell a girl when he sees her demonstrate kindness, compassion, honesty, gentleness, patience, forgiveness, or a selfless act. Has he seen her return good to someone who has been evil to her? If he has seen these acts that reflect the nature of Christ, a guy should be quick to share that observation with a girl and affirm those characteristics of Jesus. Did he see her love people no matter if they were difficult or easy to love? Has he heard her praying for people? If she is a mother, a guy should affirm her Godly instruction and encouragement toward her children. Is she teaching others the ways of God by the testimony of her life? Guys can declare these affirmations publicly so others can see his devotion to her and esteem her as well.

It is always a blessing when a guy will share the affirmations with a girl privately, too. The personal, private affirmations reach to the depths of her heart because of the intimacy that comes when you share something face to face. Sometimes that can encourage her to desire to be more like Christ and thus have the capacity to love even more. Statements that are whispered only to like "I have never been as proud as I am right now, to have you sitting next to me.' Or 'Every time I see you working with children I can tell that is what God has called you to do." Other affirmations might be seen in her work ethic or her ability to endure hard times and be patient with difficult people. Then there are statements like King Lemuel's mother taught him to say to the one that he would choose.

> *"There are many virtuous and capable women in the world,*
>
> *but you surpass them all!"*
>
> Proverbs 31:29

Those are empowering words.

Girls need to wait for the guy who affirms her; she needs this. She will never outgrow needing to be affirmed by the guy that professes to love her.

Other character traits for guys to notice and affirm are the ways she has loved him. Has she trusted him and depended on him because she believed he was able to do a certain task? Has she remembered special things that he loves and worked to provide them for him? Will she allow him to favor her, protect her or provide for her? A guy can attest to these truths and speak to her the affirmations that she needs to hear and he needs to say. Boaz affirmed and Jesus affirmed, so he we can, too.

I have a special word of encouragement to girls who did not have a father or any male authority figure in her life who affirmed her worth, talent, skills, character, or her beauty. Everyone needs to know that Psalm 139 teaches that the God of the universe put every part of her body together with purpose. God knows how many hairs are on your head. He created you in his image. Yes, you are made in the image of the Creator of the universe! Romans 5:8 says that he loves you so much that even when he knew you would sin, he died for you anyway. John 5:13 assures you that there is no greater love than when someone lays down his life for a friend, and Jesus did just that. You can trust Jesus. Follow Jesus, Give your life to Jesus. He will always be enough. His affirmations will always be true and authentic. God's Holy Spirit living in you will equip you with spiritual gifts to serve others with purpose and power. He produces fruit in your life that can actually enable you to change the word as well as bring hope to someone who is discouraged and broken hearted.

"But the Holy Spirit produces this kind of fruit in our lives: love, joy, peace, patience, kindness, goodness, faithfulness, gentleness, and self-control. There is no law against these things!"

Galations 5:22-23

YOUR OBEDIENCE AND A LIFE DRIVEN BY GOD'S TRUTH IS YOUR WAY OF AFFIRMING WHO HE IS, WHAT HE DOES AND HOW MUCH HE LOVES YOU.

"…let your good deeds shine out for all to see, so that everyone will praise your heavenly Father."

Matthew 5:16

Girls – praise and encourage the guys who are affirming the people in their life. There has been enough pointing out all of his weaknesses and failures and sin. Give the guys in your life a word of blessing for developing and practicing the discipline of affirmation when he speaks. Just saying 'thank you' is a great way to start. Tell these guys 'thank you' when you hear him affirm other girls, and girls, regarding their character and nature and not on her body or physical appearance. Let them know you noticed it and appreciate that behavior.

Praise the Lord there are guys who are raising the bar of acceptable behavior to a level of Godliness in how they treat the girls. Some guys are not falling into the shallow, temporary, self-serving trap that the world would like for them to stay bound. Be quick to give him a word of encouragement and affirmation as well. These words of praise go a long way in helping Godly behavior become permanent and life changing.

CHAPTER NINE:
DISCUSSION QUESTIONS

1. *Who models, or is a source of, AFFIRMATION in your life?*

How has that Affirmation, or LACK of it, influenced how you feel about yourself?

2. *What have you had AFFIRMED in your life?*

3. *How Does Paul AFFIRM believers in 2nd Thessalonians 1:3-4?*
    1.
    2.
    3.

4. *Can you name some people that Jesus AFFIRMED in the Bible? What did He affirm in their life or behavior?*
    Luke 7:9 –

    Mark 10:52 –

    Who else can you find in scripture that Jesus AFFIRMS?

4. Offer a genuine AFFIRMATION to 3 different people this week &
record what you said. Write what the circumstances were in which the
affirmation was given:

Also, list any ways YOU were affirmed as well:

> *Name:*   *Affirmation:*

1.

2.

.

3.

100

CHAPTER TEN:

Thing #5: Integrity

But while it's true that I am one of your family redeemers, there is another man who is more closely related to you than I am. Stay here tonight, and in the morning I will talk to him. If he is willing to redeem you, very well. Let him marry you. But if he is not willing, then as surely as the Lord lives, I will redeem you myself! Now lie down here until morning.

Ruth 3:12-13

I thought I should speak to you about it so that you can redeem it if you wish. If you want the land, then buy it here in the presence of these witnesses. But if you don't want I t, let me know right away, because I am next inline redeem it after you.

Ruth 4:4

So Boaz took Ruth into his home, and she became his wife. When he slept with her, the Lord enables her to become pregnant, and she gave birth to a son.

Ruth 4:13

Bottom line – if a guy's integrity has been lost in his relationship, none of the first four things will have much credibility. The big question is, is he really who he has led people to think he is? Do his closes friends see privately what he portrays to others publicly? This question must be answered 'yes' in all areas of his life: work, home, church or play. If there is a 'no' answer, let's pause and back up a bit in the relationship. If the people he works with, has class with, plays golf with or plays basketball or video games with, see a different guy than his wife, girlfriend, family or his church family sees, then he is a deceiver and lacking integrity.

The life of Joseph is found in the book of Genesis. He was such a great example of a man of integrity – a man resolved to surrender his thoughts and behavior to the obedience of God's commands on his life, whether anyone else saw those behaviors or not. His allegiance was to God and not to people. He was not a man who thought if he could get away with it then it was okay. Joseph was just straight up honorable and righteous.

If a guy's integrity has been lost or damaged, be encouraged; it can be restored through time with the power of God at work in his life. God did that redemptive work in lives of King David and Samson among others in God's word. Clearly, these men suffered great loss because of their lapse in moral integrity, but God, being gracious and merciful, restored them to a right relationship with himself. That restoration enabled them to do great things on God's behalf.

There are three particular demonstrations of integrity gleaned from the life of Boaz that are good for guys, as well as girls, to comprehend. It is with great encouragement that girls should watch for these attributes before entering into an exclusive relationship with a guy. He must be a guy with integrity or she will find herself in a miserable place. The following list is not made up of all the ways where integrity is demonstrated in Boaz' life, but at least some areas to begin to consider.

1. BOAZ DEMONSTRATED INTEGRITY BY BEING HONEST.

When confronted with the offer from Ruth to be his wife, he was compelled to tell her that there was a relative who was closer in the lineage than he was and therefore had first choice on the inheritance that was due him, which would be Ruth and whatever property she inherited from her late husband.

It is so amazing that Boaz's integrity trumped his feelings over her choosing him and presenting herself as willing to marry him. Instead of taking advantage of this very desirable gift of marriage to this young woman, he was quick to defer to the other relative so he was keeping the law and the ethics of family inheritance and thus bringing honor to God.

What a wonderful testimony it is for a man who is a follower of Jesus Christ to sacrifice his own personal desires for the pleasure of God's blessing.

Great respect is earned when a guy's girlfriend, wife or any of his friends, sees him make an honest move when no one else would ever know. Boaz knew there was a chance he could lose Ruth to the closer relative, but he trusted God with his future in finding a wife and therefore had no fear.

There will come at time when guys and girls will be faced with the conflict of getting something now or trusting God to provide it in an unknown future. There may be a time when the honest choice, the choice of integrity, causes them to lose out, or miss out or even reap some unfortunate consequences. This is when their faithful trust in God compels them to make the honest choice only because it pleases the Lord. And that is enough. They are convinced that God is faithful and will help them through all things. If they trust God they can wait on him to do the best things, because God always does.

Consider Abraham and his wife Sarah that we learn about in the book of Genesis. They did not trusts God enough to wait for the baby that he promised would be born to them in their old age. Waiting was just too painful, and their impatience led them into their own schemes and manipulations in how this baby would come into their lives. Personal integrity would say, 'Wait on God to provide just as he said he would.' Selfish ambitions and impatience said, 'Use whatever means you have to get that baby here, since it is taking so long.' Sarah chose her handmaid Hagar to marry Abraham so she could be the one to conceive the child they were promised. Looking at this choice it may be easy to ridicule such a foolish decision, but consider the quick start ways to God's will that many people may have used as well. Hagar and her baby, Ishmael, were evicted from the camp eventually due to Sarah's jealousy and disdain for them. Hagar's son and Sarah's son Isaac, that would be born as God had promised had, and still have, such a history of turmoil and strife. Wow, what a little integrity by being honest might have prevented.

2. The second display of integrity by Boaz was in his willingness to be accountable.

In Chapter 4 of Ruth we see Boaz deal with a legal issue of heirship with honor and the desire for accountability. Boaz searched for the man that was the closer relative of Ruth, the kinsman-redeemer, and therefore eligible to marry Ruth and inherit her land and possessions. When Boaz found him and scheduled a meeting, he called together some men from the community to gather around the negotiation table as witnesses. Boaz knew that the more witnesses there were to their discussions, the greater security and protection in the outcome.

Accountability is one of the most powerful and helpful ways of securing and maintaining a guy's integrity. It is not only for helping him become victorious over sin issues, but for helping him maintain victory over those areas as well. Accountability is not just about helping you stay out of trouble, but, to grow in Godliness in all areas of your life. You may need someone to ask you the hard questions regarding your choices in habits you need to add to your life as well as areas that need to be pruned away. A guy who is mature spiritually will let someone come alongside him and ask him about his spiritual disciplines: scripture memory, sharing the gospel with others, bible study, ministry to others, giving financially to the church and God's work as well as missional endeavors. But, he will also entrust someone to ask him about his sin struggles; "Are you stealing from your work place?", "Are you cheating in any school work?",, "Are you maintaining purity with your girlfriend?", "Did you look at any pornographic material this week?", "Have you asked forgiveness from

notes:

the person you offended"?, "Is there any relationship at work that is, or has the potential to be, a threat to the integrity of your marriage?"

It is not only good for a guy to have his spiritual mentors ask him the hard questions, but some new questions are helpful as well. After learning these 5 Things you might have someone ask you: "How are you showing her favor?", "What have you provided for her this week? Did you do anything for her that others would see and thing 'He sure does love her!'", "Did you protect her body, spirit or character from any who might bring her harm in those areas? What specific actions did you take to give her that protection?", "List for me three ways you have affirmed her through encouragement and contributing to her strength of character and her walk of faith.", "Were there any moments this week that you were challenged to compromise your integrity? Not only in your relationship, but at work or hanging out with your friends in any environment?"

What a powerful and effective demonstration of integrity is when you allow yourself to be accountable to someone.

3. THE THIRD ACT OF INTEGRITY WE SEE IN THE LIFE OF BOAZ IS HIS PURITY.

Merriam Webster defines purity as a lack of dirty or harmful substances, as well as, a lack of guilt or evil thoughts. I find the working so crucial in Chapter 4 of Ruth regarding Boaz's relationship with Ruth. The scripture says he married Ruth, then he slept with her, and the Lord gave them a son. Note that God does indeed have an order by which couples should live their lives regarding sexual intimacy. This text seems to say that Boaz and Ruth stayed with that order. If guys and girls want to engage in a sexual activity, they should be married first. This is spiritual integrity.

Challenges to spiritual integrity regarding sexual purity start way back at creation. Clearly from reading the Mosaic Law, the same perversions of God's design we see today were going on in that day as well. Scripture is clear that sexual activity is reserved for marriage. All sexual activity outside of that covenant relationship is impure and therefore sinful. God's command to everyone is –

"And now dear brothers and sisters, one final thing. Fix your thoughts on what is true, and honorable, and right, and pure, and lovely, and admirable. Think about things that are excellent and worthy of praise."

Philippians 4:8

God tells us we should get rid of the things that cause impurity.

"So put to death the sinful, earthly things lurking within you. Have nothing to do with sexual immorality, impurity, lust, and evil desires. Don't be greedy, for a greedy person is an idolater, worshiping the things of this world."
Colossians 3:5

There is just no room for compromise in the area of purity. Anything that robs the mind or a life of its cleanness or clarity, especially in relationships, should be cast aside. God's word teaches how to be free of these sins.

"Therefore, since we are surrounded by such a huge crowd of witnesses to the life of faith, let us trip off every weight that slows us down, especially the sin that so easily trips us up. And let us run with endurance the race God has set before us. We do this by keeping our eyes on Jesus, the champion who initiates and perfects our faith."
Hebrews 12:1-2

Guys, you must earn the respect you want. Authentic, unshakeable and enduring respect comes to a guy whose life exemplifies integrity. Respectful behavior can be demanded in some environments, but what a cheap respect.

God's character can flourish in your life through the power of the Holy Spirit. He enables a guy to have integrity,

108

because he is the same yesterday, today and forever. He is who he says he is.

"And I am certain that God, who began the good work within you, will continue his work until it is finally finished on the day when Christ Jesus returns." Philippians

1:6

Job was a man in the bible who loved God and worshipped him always. He was tested in life like no other. He lost his children his crops, his animals and his health. His wife and some of his close friends tried to quench his spirit and trust in God by saying that it was probably his fault these tragic things happened and this was God's punishment. They urged him to forget about God – even curse him. However, in the book of Job, chapters 1-5, Job was commended for his integrity, and God said Job was blameless, and that there was no one like him! One of his friends acknowledged Job's integrity.

"Doesn't your reverence for God give you confidence? Doesn't your life of integrity give you hope?" Job 4:6

James admonishes everyone to be people of integrity when committing to do something. A person's word should be the seal of assurance. He admonishes everyone in this when he wrote in James 5:12, *"But most of all, my brothers and sisters, never take an oath, by heaven or earth or anything else. Just say a simple yes or no, so that you will not sin and be condemned."*

The testimony of a guy's integrity is secured when he is the same wherever he is and not just in the presence of those he is trying to fool.

"So whether we are here in this body or away from this body, our goal is to please him. For we must all stand before Christ to be judged."

2nd Corinthians 5:9-10

Boaz gives guys three strong areas to evaluate in their lives. The goal of personal integrity in honesty, accountability and purity is not only noble, but obeying the commands of Christ.

What about the other areas of his life? The trust he earns from a girl generates an abiding, adoring kind of love in their relationship. When she trusts him, he has earned a most valuable gift.

THE GUY SHE NEEDS TO WAIT TO MARRY IS
FULL OF INTEGRITY. BE THAT GUY.

CHAPTER TEN:
DISCUSSION QUESTIONS

1. *On a scale of 1-10, with 10 being the most important, how big of a deal is it that these people have integrity? Why?*

Friends –

Girlfriend/Boyfriend –

Parents –

Teachers –

Ministers –

Political leaders –

2. *Read these verses below and find these 2 things:*

> *1. Underline what ACTION or BEHAVIOR is required from you that demonstrates integrity.*

> *2. Circle the BENEFITS that come when you obey the integrity requirements.*

Psalm 25:20-21

"Guard my soul and deliver me: Do not let me be ashamed, for I take refuge in you. Let integrity and uprightness preserve me, for I wait for you."

Psalm 26:1-3

"Dismiss all charges against me, Lord, for I have walked in my integrity, and I have trusted in the Lord without wavering. Examine me, O Lord, and try me; test my mind and my heart. For your loving kindness is before my eyes, and I have walked in your truth."

Proverbs 10:9

"He who walks in integrity walks securely, but he who perverts his ways will be found out"

Proverbs 11:3

"The integrity of the upright will guide them, but the crookedness of the treacherous will destroy them."

Proverbs 20:7, 11   vs 7

"A righteous man who walks in his integrity – How blessed are his sons after him."

Vs. 11 "It is by his deeds that a young person distinguishes himself if his conduct is pure and right."

Titus 2:6-7

"In the same way, urge the young men to behave carefully, taking life seriously. And here you yourself must be an example to them of good deeds of every kind. Let everything you do reflect your love of the truth and the fact that you are in dead serious about it."

114

CHAPTER ELEVEN:
Redeemed

Have you realized yet that Ruth is the foreshadow of us? Just like Boaz was the "kinsman-redeemer" and therefore a foreshadow of what Jesus Christ would be to us, Ruth is the foreshadow of who we would be before Jesus Christ redeemed us.

When we were a stranger to the things of God, we were not part of the family of God and had not learned of who Jesus was or what he had to offer us, God sent Jesus Christ to earth to show us who God was and invited us to the table. Just like Boaz invited Ruth and she became part of his family, we are invited by God to join his family. That is the good news that Jesus brings to the whole world! We can become part of his family and thus live with him for eternity when we die, because he redeemed us!

Boaz restored Ruth's status in the community when he made her his wife. This redemption was crucial to the family. Just as it is with us in our faith family of God. Jesus restores all that was lost and could not be fixed. Our inability to permanently change those things about us that keep us feeling guilty and shamed, stuck in habits and behaviors that seem insurmountable, and the judgement that comes with all of that – is redeemed by the power of God and the act of Jesus dying and shedding blood to pay for all of our sins. We can't wash it away, but Jesus can. If you have never given your life to Jesus, you can trust him. He is your redeemer and is worthy of every ounce of your devotion and worship and obedience.

Naomi and Ruth found themselves in a desperate place when they moved back to Bethlehem as widows. All that they owned and even their own status as contributing members of the community were in jeopardy. They needed someone related to them to restore, or redeem, their property. Which meant they must take one of them to be their wife as well. How gracious that God would send them this wonderful, kind "kinsman redeemer" in Boaz. He loved Ruth. Because he loved her and wanted her for his wife, he was able to redeem her. His agreement to take possession of all she owned and take her as his wife brought new hope, new joy and a new future. Just like Jesus does for us.

For the guy that has found himself at the end of this book feeling unfit or discouraged at his poor application of these 5 Things be encouraged by this great news. You, too, have a Redeemer. God's word says that no one can measure up to the example that Jesus set in himself. Everyone is born with nature that will choose his own interests and selfish desire every time left to his own choices. People are spiritually lost, destined to fail until God sent a Redeemer, the one who would buy back and restore value to all people through his shed blood on the cross at Calvary. Because of his great sacrifice, everyone has been given a hope and a promise that you can be more than conquerors over the hurdles and complications that this temporary world presents. The whole world needed a Redeemer. Families, marriages and all relationship need to be redeemed. You can put your trust in God right now by confessing that you need a rescuer, you need a redeemer that can restore all that has been broken. Surrender your life to Jesus Christ and get in his word to find life's answers and master plan for how to live your life abundantly. You can tell him now.

Guys will need to understand that, in order for these 5 Things to be fully developed, fluid, rich and maximized in their effectiveness, they must know the designer and sustainer of all life and health and strength. That designer and sustainer is our loving, sovereign God.

Have you considered building that tower? That wonderful tower of a committed relationship? Have you counted the cost of making that kind of commitment, and believe you have the resources to complete it? Then you must acknowledge that the only way you can know God is through his son Jesus Christ. He has such a wonderful plan for your life. He takes all that we have ever experienced, good and bad, and works it out for our good. He loves us so much.

notes:

God's power and precepts enable you to live out this lifelong commitment. Knowing him is crucial in your development as a great boyfriend and one day, a great husband. Everything worth anything involves a relationship.

For a girl who is considering dating someone or wants to get married, please wait on the guy that demonstrates a heart for being a man of the 5 Things. These 5 Things are not formed from a survey or based on the opinions of others; they are straight from the word of God and they are timeless. Find a guy who lives these things out in his life already or at least you see him working on incorporating them into his life.

When a guy begins building this wonderful relationship tower and considers the divinely appointed role as the leader, it will require tremendous discipline. If he goes into a relationship, and certainly marriage, with selfish motives and a survey-based agenda, he will only last as long as the cultural trends and the popular voice will allow.

notes:

However, if he wants to go the distance in completing the tower with all of its unexpected interruptions, extra expenses, and challenges, get acquainted with the one who can enable them to complete that tower. If they will surrender to the requirements written and established by the builder and designer of relationships himself, the Holy Spirit will train, correct, and equip them in leading their wives in a manner that is pleasing to the Lord and can last a lifetime.

Consider finding a mentor. Find a man of integrity who you have seen demonstrate these 5 Things in their marriages, toward their children and in their work place and ask him to teach you.

To the guys who are following God and living out the character of Christ and wanting to please him, carry on! It is going to be great when that girls meets you one day and discovers at everything she was hoping, praying, and waiting for proved to be so worth it!

It is crucial that a guy determines in his heart to live out these 5 Things long before he is in a committed relationship. Learn them and live them out now. Practice these things now in ways that are appropriate for his age and the level of his relationship. These are disciplines that show girls now what his goals are in becoming a faithful boyfriend and ultimately a faithful husband. She needs to see that he has become well acquainted with the character of God by living out these disciplines to his friends and family members long before he is ready to commit to her. "For God is working in you, giving you the desire and the power to do what pleases him." Philippians 2:13

I am praying, and I ask everyone who reading this book to pray with me, that guys and girls all over the world will look to the infallible word of God for the standards why which they will live. Any other standard of measure will leave them unsatisfied, confused and disillusioned. Enduring, lifelong marriages can happen. When you sit down and consider the requirements, the cost for building this tower that must hold for a lifetime, remember it can be done. A forever marriage will be a reality when obedience to God's plan, found in the bible, is your plan. Read it, memorize it and live it out loud.

Guys - Favor, Provision, Protection, Affirmation and Integrity are part of the blueprint you need to be developing in your life. Start now. These 5 Things don't just show up in your life because you get a girlfriend or get married. The come from hard work and paying the price of what it means to lay down your life for her, and knowing that the only way you could ever do that is through the power of God.

Girls – these 5 Things create profile of the guy you need to wait on before dating them and for sure marrying them. Many hours, days and sometimes years, have been lost on relationships that cost you joy and peace in your spirit and in your mind and even sometimes in your body. Pray for patience, discernment, and a resolve straight from the heart of God, that you are, indeed, willing to wait for a guy who treats you the way Jesus does. Why?

BECAUSE YOU ARE WORTHY
OF ALL THAT GOD HAS IN STORE.

"For you know that God paid a ransom (redeemed you) to save you from
the empty life you inherited from your ancestors. And the ransom he
paid was not mere gold or silver. It was the precious blood of Christ, the
sinless spotless Lamb of God. God chose him as your ransom long before
the world began, but he has now revealed him to you in these last days.
Through Christ you have come to trust in God. And you have placed
your faith and hope in God because he raised Christ from the dead and
gave him great glory. You were cleansed from your sins when you obeyed
the truth, so now you must show sincere love to each other as brothers
and sisters. Love each other deeply with all your heart. For you have been
born again, but not to a life that will quickly end. Your new life will last
forever because it comes from the eternal, living word of God."

1st Peter 1:18-23

CHAPTER ELEVEN:
DISCUSSION QUESTIONS

1. *Have you ever collected something or found something that could be taken to a store and redeemed for money? Ex. Baseball cards, coke bottles/ glass, prize ticket, etc.*

2. *Who determines how much something is worth? Why?*

3. *How much do you feel you are worth? What do you think is your most valuable asset?*

4. *With Jesus being your Redeemer, he is the one that determined how much YOU are worth. What does scripture teach about your worth to God?*

5. *Why is it important to know WHO redeemed you and WHY He did?*

6. *Of the 5 Things you have studied in this book, which of them do you feel you need God to refine more in your life?*

What are some practical ways you might begin to grow in this area?

Which of them do you feel more affirmation from God?

FAQ'S

The questions I have included in this list are just a few of the many questions that have been asked multiple times over the years. Most provoked by the principles I have taught and written about in my book "5 Things". I pray they will help you in your pursuit of a healthy, vibrant and fulfilling relationship as well. Remember – it really is only Jesus that can satisfy the deepest longings of your soul. Another human being can only share in that satisfaction.

PRAYER:

1. Is it appropriate to pray together when you are still dating? Does it develop a spiritual intimacy that should be reserved for marriage?

Answer:

Prayer will develop an intimacy with God. Praying together gets messed up only if it is made to be a part of your "dating package" requirements. Prayer, in its purest form, is like breathing – it is a moment by moment conversation with your Savior. Scripture teaches us to "pray without ceasing" (I Thessalonians 5:17). Jesus prayed everyday, alone (Mark 1:35), with others (Matthew 19:13), and for others (John 17:6-26). So, it seems to me, that when you are dating someone or not, you pray together because you pray already.

2. Do you think we should pray with a boyfriend/girlfriend? Or is that meant for marriage?

Answer:

Most of this is answered in Question #1. However, I am curious as to where this philosophy of "prayer only being meant for marriage" comes from? There is no Biblical precedent for this being an issue for marriage only. We need each other to be praying for each other. I think the mistake here, is making "praying together" a checked item for dating, like it is a spiritual standard of behavior for a special relationship. You don't have to pray with each other at all – there is no command of scripture for you to pray with your girlfriend, fiancé' or wife, but, there is a command, and plenty of examples, that you should pray – all the time, anytime, for people, for yourself, in your closet, with a few, with a group, with boldness, with humility & in Jesus' name. This should keep your prayer life vibrant and active, organic and constant.

3. How can I make my prayer life better when praying for my future spouse? Is there scripture to support specifically what needs prayer?

Answer:

Jesus gave us an example of how we should pray in Matthew 6:5-13. Examine those elements and make them a part of your specific prayer time. You also have been given a huge measure of grace in being able to approach the throne of God to ask and receive in Hebrews 4:14-16

Regarding your question "can I ask for a specific thing regarding a wife/husband?" – There is an example of that in a passage of scripture about Abraham's worker that was commissioned to go find a wife for Isaac, Abraham's son. Abraham gave some general directives about who to look for and where etc., but then as the worker traveled to the territory he was to look for a woman for Isaac in, he began to ask God for some very specific signs regarding his mission. You can read these in Genesis 24:12-14. I am not suggesting that you pray this way, but I am just pointing out that there is a precedent in scripture for making specific requests.

4. What is one way to pray for a woman? How do I pray for her?
   Answer:

   * Pray the scripture.

   * Pray she will obey the commands of Christ as a follower of Christ. If she doesn't have a personal relationship with Jesus Christ, then pray that she will come to know and trust Christ and give her life to Him by faith.

   * Pray specifically that she will mature in her spiritual gift(s) from God as found in Ephesians 4:7, 11-12 and I Corinthians 12:4-11 and Romans 12:4-8.

   * Pray for her to develop the nature & character traits of the virtuous woman in Proverbs 31:10-31

WAITING:

Do you not know? Have you not heard? The Everlasting God, the Lord, the Creator of the ends of the earth does not become weary or tired. His understanding is inscrutable. He gives strength to the weary, and to him who lacks might He increases power. Though youths grow weary and tired, and vigorous young men stumble badly, yet those who wait for the Lord will gain new strength; they will mount up with wings like eagles, they will run and not get tired, they will walk and not become weary.

Isaiah 40:28-31 (NASB)

1. How do you wait for the person God has for you?

Answer:

I know what you are asking, but my answer is going to re-direct you. The way you wait for the person, is to wait for God. Think of a waiter in a restaurant. Why are they called waiters? Because they are waiting to hear whatever it is the ones they are serving need them to do. They come by often to see how they can serve. They also come when they are summoned. Your waiter will replenish, refill and try to do everything they can to meet your needs. I think this is a beautiful illustration of what we do when we are waiting on God to respond to our petitions and answer the desires of our heart. You serve him – that's how you wait. Read God's word and see what he wants you to do, talk to him and ask if there is anything he needs from you. Then be about meeting those requests, commands and directions he gives you.

It's not an idle wait, it's an active, hopeful, energetic wait. So my encouragement to you is to focus your waiting on the one who knows everything you need and desire to have. Be about the Lords business and obeying his call on your life. That is when waiting gets really fun.

2. What are some good ways to be patient when waiting?

Answer:

* Drink in all the truths of God's word. Memorize the principles, stories and scripture verses that will equip you to live a Godly life and be ready for any occasion to give a reason for the hope that is in you which is Jesus Christ.

* Study the characteristics of a Godly man or woman that we are given in the Bible. You do not have to wait for marriage to be a man or woman of God. You can, and need to, be that now.

*Love people – just give your life away. Look for ways to serve in missions or any ministry area where you see a need, whether in your church, community or in lands far away.

3. How would I go about waiting on a girl who may not exhibit some of the traits you teach about that are in the Bible?

Answer:

I am hearing you say you want to wait on a girl that does not exhibit all of the Biblical traits and disciplines a wife/woman should have. If this is a correct understanding – I am thankful you are waiting. Refer to my answer in the question about how to wait. I think you will get an idea about how to wait from that section. However, while you are waiting for God, I encourage you to pray for this special woman in your life to learn from older believers and be disciple in her walk with Christ, so that she can mature and be strengthened in these areas of weakness. Remember, no one is going to be perfectly mature in all aspects of their spiritual disciplines. This is what we spend a lifetime developing and changing and bringing under the authority of God. But, what you need to see is a life lived out in pursuit of these. If she is faithfully keeping her eyes on Jesus and desiring to change the weaker areas by letting them be refined by Gods workmanship, then carry on. "I don't mean to say that I have already achieved these things or that I have already reached perfection. But I press on to possess that perfection for which Christ Jesus first possessed me." Philippians 3:12

4. How can I be sure a man's heart is truly in pursuit of my heart? I want to wait on the man whom God has saved for me, but how can I be sure I'm not missing out on the right man?

Answer:

Your best assurance will come when you observe the fruit of the Spirit listed in Galatians 5:22: love, joy, peace, patience, kindness, goodness, faithfulness, gentleness and self-control, in his life. Look for the "5 Things" taught in this book. These are Biblical disciplines gleaned from the life of Boaz in the book of Ruth, which are also found in Jesus. Watch for these and see if they are exercised authentically and continuously, and not just toward you, but you see these graces extended toward all people. But dear friend, marrying someone will always involve a measure of faith. Not a blind faith, but a faith that is grounded in what you see in his life now will be what you see fourteen years from now.

Regarding "the man God has saved for me" and not "missing out on the right man" – there is some conflict built in here. If God has indeed saved someone in particular for you, he is faithful to keep his promises. He would not relinquish his selection for you, and therefore, your fear of missing out on that right one is unfounded.

However, my encouragement to you is that you be diligent, prayerful & watchful for a man that is living out his faith with integrity. A man whose life speaks to the fact that he is a man after God's heart. At the same time you need to be developing your faith walk as well. Don't let fear entrap you. Scripture teaches us to "Take delight in the Lord, and he will give you your heart's desires." Psalm 37:4 This passage is in the middle of a chapter about God's provisions when dealing with an enemy. I think this promise is based on his perfect, unchanging character and therefore still a promise we can claim as well. So delight in him and you will find that the desires of your heart will begin to look like the desires of his.

PAST HURTS:

1. What does a woman who has been hurt by men in the past do, if it's almost impossible for her to trust a man to lead her? Even Godly men have failed her. How can I help her?

Answer:

The first response that came to my mind regarding what she should do after being hurt is to forgive. While that may not be the answer she wanted to hear, Jesus says "If you forgive those who sin against you, your heavenly Father will forgive you." Matthew 6:14 It is clearly commanded that we must forgive, if we want to be forgiven. And we so desperately need to be forgiven.

The other thought that comes to my mind is how huge the price is that we pay for sin. Not only when we are the offender, but when we have been offended by sin as well. It has such grave consequences on a person's heart.

Because of the lack of integrity and demonstration of godliness she has experienced from men who claim to be Christ followers, she feels it is impossible to trust a man to lead her. This now has rooted in her life and has become a sin which entangles her in the web of Satan's lies. It has the potential to throw her off course in the design that God has established for a marriage. The enemy knows that the design of God for marriage is that the husband lead. So the enemy is now tempting her to sin by not wanting to trust him to lead, and thus hesitating to let him lead. When Godly men sin, when they have failed to live up to the standard of holiness and integrity that he is called to, it causes someone to stumble. Jesus has a very strong warning to all of us when he taught his disciples that *"One day Jesus said to his disciples, 'There will always be temptations to sin, but what sorrow awaits the person who does the tempting!" Luke 17:1*

Tell her to keep her eyes fixed on Jesus. Learn about his character and the way he teaches you to love and what that looks like. Start with 1st Corinthians 13. Tell her to pray for healing and rebuke the lies that Satan would have her believe, then walk with confidence in the freedom that the Holy Spirit of God gives. Tell her not to listen to the whispers of the ones that would keep her bound to a hopeless future. Live out your life with purpose and intention to share the good news of Jesus Christ with others, love people and learn how to be friends with guys in your life. God has and will continue to raise up great men of God who want to be like him and they want to love people like he does. They want to treat their girlfriends with honor and grace. They want to be faithful husbands and raise families that serve the Lord. Please, tell her to wait for one of those men while she continues to serve Jesus.

2. I am incapable of giving a guy my heart because even the most awesome guy I have dated has cheated on me, etc. How will I be able to love someone when God puts him into my life, because I am now cold-hearted towards men?

Answer:

It is devastating when trust is broken. That deep wound that seems like it will never go away is not too complex for an omnipotent God. 2nd Corinthians 5:17 tells us he is the restorer of all things. He restores beauty from ashes (Isaiah 61:3), he also totally renews your mind, when you offer him your life as a living sacrifice (Romans 12:2). The cold-hearted feeling you have, as well as the feeling of being "incapable" of loving again is not what you are left to be in God's design of things. In Ezekiel 37 we read a story where God takes the prophet Ezekiel to look at a valley of dry bones which represents the lost hope of God's people. God tells Ezekiel that when he speaks the Truth that God has given him to speak to the dry bones, that they will be restored to life. Sure enough, when Ezekiel speaks those words to the bones laying there on the dry, parched ground their skin and muscles begin to be repaired and they begin to breathe again and in moments they are all restored to life and health. They did not just have their life and hope restored, but we are told they stood up as a mighty army! This can be you, too, precious friend. As a child of God, you are not destined to stay in the valley with a hopeless spirit, incapable of loving a man with joyful anticipation of a lifetime together in an enduring marriage. Listen to the Truth and walk in it – even if you don't feel it. That is a walk of faith. Walk in the knowledge that God is faithful and he will always keep His promises. (Please read the answer to question 1 in this category for more truths from God's word regarding your question.)

3. How do you go about speaking about past relationships with your significant other?

Answer:

Very carefully.

If you have asked the Lord to forgive you, then you are walking in forgiveness and purity that his sacrificial blood was spilled for. Therefore, it is not for forgiveness or to be redeemed that you would share any of the issues of your past with anyone. That has been accomplished by Christ alone. However, any issues that could have a direct impact on the future health of your relationship, especially a marriage, should be shared with the discretion that the Holy Spirit allows. For example, if you have had multiple sexual partners, or engaged in taking drugs where there was sharing of needles or any other behaviors or addictions that could impact your emotional or physical health in the future, these need to be revealed. I think the honorable time to share these past issues of your life should be shared while you are still at the friend level. This disclosure, while still friends, enables a measure of grace to the one listening and then they can determine if these issues of your past are deal breakers for them. They need time to pray through their concerns and convictions and then choose whether to continue progressing in this relationship. You both need a future filled with peace and joy even if you decide that staying friends is how God will define your relationship at this time. James says to "Confess you sins to each other and pry for each other so that you may be healed. The earnest prayer of a righteous person has great power and produces wonderful results." James 5:16 The bottom line is to listen to the prompting of the Holy Spirit and follow his lead concerning when and how much should be shared. He is always right.

4. *Being a Christian who has messed up in regards to purity how do you come back from that?*

Answer:

You come back from moral failure through the power of an almighty God that has shed his redemptive blood for you. It is Christ alone that enables you to come back from that failure with a heart that is as white as snow. This is what redemption is. God buys you back! Anything else that you have done that falls short of God's desire for us is covered under the blood of Jesus that was shed for us on Calvary. God's word reminds us *"... without the shedding of blood there is no forgiveness of sin."* Hebrews 9:22

I hope that you will find more help in the answers already given. I loved answering this question, because it prompts the telling of the good news of the redemption and salvation we have in Christ Jesus. I praise God all the time that I am not bound in the chains of the sins of my past. You don't have to be bound, either. *"So if the Son makes you free, you will be free indeed."* (John 8:36 NASB)

How Can I be 'Born Again'?

If you want to know how you can be born again and become a Christ follower. Please read these passages of scripture. Then talk to God and tell him of your desire to turn from your sins and give your life to him in obedience to his command.

John 3:1-16

Jesus says we must be born-again.

Jesus says God loved us so much that he sent his son, Jesus, to die in our place for the sins that we commit,

Romans 5:8

God showed us how much he loves us, in that even though we were still sinning, Christ died for us.

Romans 10:9

If you openly declare that Jesus is Lord and believe in your heart that God raised him from the dead, you will be saved (born-again).

Luke 5:31-32

Jesus tells us that just as a person needs a doctor when they are sick, sinners, like all of us are, need to repent. Repent means to turn away completely from sin and go the other way. And that is why God sent Jesus to earth– to show us who we can turn toward after we turn away from our sin.

Philippians 2:13

You are not the one that has to "power up" to change your life from sinful behavior to righteous behavior. This scripture teaches us that it is God who will be at work within you to help you not only desire to do what pleases him, but also the ability to do what pleases him.

JESUS WILL ALWAYS BE ENOUGH FOR WHATEVER YOU NEED

Kathy Nelson, FOUNDER,
DIRECTOR OF SPEAK IT MINISTRIES

AUTHOR OF "5 THINGS"

WWW.SPEAKITMINISTRIES.COM
FACEBOOK
TWITTER - @CCKATHY
INSTAGRAM - KATHYBNELSON